A
Harlequin
Romance

OTHER
Harlequin Romances
by BELINDA DELL

1162—ISLAND OF LOVE
1193—HOSPITAL IN KASHMIR
1371—DANCING ON MY HEART
1407—NEXT STOP GRETNA
1475—THE VERMILION GATEWAY

Many of these titles are available at your local bookseller,
or through the Harlequin Reader Service.

For a free catalogue listing all available Harlequin Romances,
send your name and address to:

HARLEQUIN READER SERVICE,
M.P.O. Box 707, Niagara Falls, N.Y. 14302
Canadian address: Stratford, Ontario, Canada.

or use order coupon at back of book.

FLOWERS FOR THE FESTIVAL

by

BELINDA DELL

HARLEQUIN BOOKS

TORONTO
WINNIPEG

Original hard cover edition published in 1972
by Mills & Boon Limited, 17-19 Foley Street,
London   W1A 1DR, England

© Belinda Dell 1972

Harlequin edition published September, 1972

SBN 373-01623-9

Printed in Canada

1623

CHAPTER I

Lindy had just settled herself down with a tray of coffee and a novel she had been intending to read for months, when the doorbell rang. The unexpected sound made her jerk her hand so that the coffee spilled a few hot drops on her skirt from the spout of the pot.

'Ouch!' she said as the sensation penetrated through the tweed to her leg. But otherwise she made no response; she didn't want to struggle out of her chair and into the hall. She hoped the caller would go away. She wasn't expecting anyone. No meter-readers were due, no repair men had been asked to come and look at the lopsided picture on the TV set, no bakers, grocers or milkman were awaited. Her flatmate Julia, as she left for the office that morning, had said with satisfaction that Lindy could sit quietly and undisturbed all day, resting her injured ankle and doing herself a world of good.

So Lindy told herself that whoever was at the door had better just go back to where he came from, and began to pour her coffee.

The buzzer sounded again. Exasperated, she put down the pot. The hand pressing the bell was very purposeful—the sound went on for several unbroken seconds.

'All right!' she remarked in a grumbling tone. 'All right, I'm coming.'

There wasn't the slightest chance that the caller could hear this, for he or she was downstairs in the hall of the old Knightsbridge house whereas Lindy was up in what had once been the attics. And to prove it, by the time she had laid aside the coffee-tray, heaved herself out of her armchair and hobbled on her plaster-encased foot to the hall, the buzzer was sounding again, even more imperiously than before.

When the tall narrow house was converted into flats the architect had realized that the occupants of the upper floors might not always want to answer the outside door. So a communications system had been installed rather on the lines of a baby-alarm, with a microphone in the hallway and inside the doors of the three top flats.

'Who is it?' Lindy inquired.

There was a startled sound from below as the visitor heard this disembodied voice. Then, as he discovered the little grating labelled 'Speak here', the reply came.

'This is Arnold.'

Lindy jerked her head back from the speaker-grating in her flat as if it had bitten her.

'Who?' she said faintly.

Even distorted by the mike, the voice carried the exasperation she had heard so often in the past.

'Don't be an idiot, Lindy. This is your brother Arnold.'

There was a long pause.

'Lindy? Lindy, how do I open this confounded door?'

'Just a minute,' she replied. She pushed the button that released the catch of the downstairs door. 'Now,' she said.

And now he was climbing the four flights of stairs towards her—her brother Arnold, the last man in the world she'd expected. And perhaps the last man she wanted to see.

She wouldn't answer the door. When he got to the top floor, she would tell him to go away. She didn't want to talk to him. It was two years since they had exchanged any words; two years in which they had sent each other dutiful Christmas and birthday cards but not a single letter, two years in which she had learned to live a life of her own.

But of course when he spoke again, rather breathlessly outside the door of the flat, she let him in.

'Hello,' she said. It seemed inadequate after a separation of some twenty-eight months, but she couldn't bring herself to say 'Welcome' or 'Nice to see you'.

He came in, frowning. 'Confounded stairs,' he

grumbled. 'Why on earth do you have to live on a level with Mount Everest?'

Although she was tall for a girl, he loomed over her. He was well over six foot in height, and broad in proportion. His heavy-rimmed glasses gave him a sombre look; as usual his hair looked as if it had not seen a comb for days.

'Well,' he said, 'how's the ankle?'

Lindy turned a perplexed gaze upon him. 'How did you know about my ankle?' she said.

'Some girl wrote to me.' He fished in his jacket pocket, to produce a dog-eared postcard which he held up for her to read.

Feel I should tell you Lindy broke her ankle this morning, and has been taken into St George's Hospital. Yrs, Julia Jenkins,' Lindy read.

'Oh, the idiot,' she said in exasperation. 'They only kept me in overnight!'

'So I gathered when I rang them yesterday.'

'You rang them?'

'Naturally. And they told me—'

'But why?'

'Because I'm your brother. Oh, you mean, why did I ring, not why did they give me information? Oh, well, the answer's still the same. You *are* the only relative I have, just as I am the only relative you have. So naturally I wanted to know how you were.'

'But what are you doing *here*?' Lindy asked, still at a loss.

Arnold shrugged his shoulders about in his shabby jacket. 'Are we going to conduct this conversation standing in the hall, or could we sit down like civilized people?' he countered.

She felt herself flushing with embarrassment, and was furious with herself. How could she let him put her in the wrong so quickly, when for more than two years she had been in sensible control of herself and her own actions and managed quite well?

'This way,' she said. She tried not to lean heavily on

the stick as she led the way into the little slope-roofed living-room. ' Do sit down. That's the most comfortable chair.'

It was a modern leather rocker. Arnold gave it a glance of disdain before sitting in the armchair she had vacated. He eyed the tray on the low table alongside.

' Coffee?' she offered, making as if to move towards it.

' Let me,' he said.

He poured half a cup, looked at it, paused. ' It looks pretty cold. I'll heat it up. Which is the kitchen?'

' That way.'

As he bore the tray away, she reflected that the situation was typical. Within two minutes of ringing her doorbell, Arnold was taking charge of her life again.

In the past she had never thought to question it. Arnold was the clever one of the family, the shining light; intelligent, able and well-organized, he had dominated not only Lindy but her mother and father. When they died in a holiday train crash abroad, it was to Arnold that she had turned for comfort and security. At sixteen she had been a shy and rather reticent girl, still in need of a father-figure. The eleven-year age gap between herself and Arnold enabled him to fill that role for her, so that for the next five years of her life she had accepted his views, bowed to his judgement, kept house for him and scarcely thought to question the rightness of this regime.

It was only when she was twenty-one that panic seized her. It was *her* life. She had a right to live it in her own way. And so, two years previously, in the month of December, she had packed up and left. She had run away, leaving a letter for Arnold to find when he came home from the college in Cambridge where he was holding a tutorial. A silly, cowardly, juvenile act—one of which she was not at all proud when she thought about it now, although at the time she had felt it to be the only course open to her. The alternative would have been to face her brother, to have a showdown: and two years ago

8

Doralinda Elizabeth Gramont had not had the strength of character she now had.

Or did she have it now? Here she stood, hesitating and feeling uncertain just because Arnold had reappeared in her life.

Well, it was understandable. She was taken by surprise. And, truth to tell, she didn't feel too good; her ankle pained her and she still had some bruises from the fall. It was no wonder she felt a little shaky.

She lowered herself into the rocker that Arnold had rejected, and realized at once that that was a mistake—the backward swing of the chair brought both feet off the floor unexpectedly, causing a shaft a pain in her left leg.

'Here, let me help you,' said Arnold, reappearing at her side as she struggled to get up again. He helped her to another chair, found a footstool and a cushion on which to prop her injured foot, then went to fetch the coffee.

'How did it happen?' he inquired as he sat down with the tray alongside him.

'I was on a pair of steps hanging a garland—'

'And you fell off.'

'I was knocked off. One of the catering staff backed into the steps so that they rocked, and I went over on to the floor.'

Her brother raised thick eyebrows. 'Where on earth was this?' he inquired. 'It all sounds very odd. Some church fête?'

'It was in the Connaught Rooms,' she replied rather coldly. 'I was doing the flower decoration for a wedding reception.'

'Good heavens!' He brought her a cup. 'Sugar? No?' He gave a half-smile. 'You used to take sugar.'

'I've changed. A person can change a lot in two years, Arnold.'

'Quite so.' He went back to his place, sat down again, and put two heaped spoons of brown sugar in his own coffee. 'Is that what you do, then? Flower arranging?'

9

' Yes.'

' Mm.' He took a sip, paused with the cup still in mid-air as he surveyed the room. ' Seems to pay well,' he observed.

' It pays very well if you're good at it. And I am good at it.'

' Well done, you. Who would have thought it?' He drank appreciatively, then said, ' You haven't a biscuit, I suppose? I'm awfully peckish. Didn't stop for break-fast on the way south, you know.'

' Oh, of course! I should have offered—' Once again Lindy started to get up and once again he forestalled her.

' Just tell me where to find them.'

' On the shelf above the fridge. In the canister marked " Biscuits ".'

' Well, that seems logical.' He came back in a moment with the open container clasped under one arm, and a mouthful of biscuit crumbs.

' Do you mean,' Lindy asked, not altogether willing to ask the question but impelled by curiosity, ' that you drove overnight from Edinburgh?'

He nodded.

' But why?'

He munched for some moments before replying. ' Ah well, there are times when a certain course of action seems called for. You and I, little sister, have lived in a state of suspended animation long enough. This seemed the moment to resume diplomatic relations. And I must say,' he added, gazing into the biscuit tin and hunting around for another lemon cream, ' that I'm glad I came. It's quite clear you're not managing too well on your own.'

' Good heavens, Arnold, I've only been home from the hospital twenty-four hours! I haven't had time to get used to being in plaster yet.'

' How long d'you think it's going to take you?'

' Oh, I don't know. A couple of days, I expect.'

' And how long is the plaster to stay on?'

' Three or four weeks, the surgeon said.'

Arnold put the tin down and went back to his coffee.

' That's quite a while. Will you be able to do your flower arranging during that time?'

' No . . . o. A few things, perhaps. But in the first place I shan't be able to drive for a while and that makes it difficult about getting to market and taking supplies to the situation. And of course it limits my mobility—I shan't be climbing any step-ladders for a week or so.'

' So you'll be at home here?'

' I expect so.'

' A bit dull, isn't it? Cooped up here under the eaves beside the sparrows?'

She knew in her heart that this was true, but she wouldn't admit it to him. She didn't want to acknowledge the fact that the idea of having to hobble up and down these four flights of stairs for the next few weeks was a prospect of dismay.

' It'll be all right,' she said.

' You must be joking. You'll die of boredom and loneliness. This girl that wrote to me—she's out all day, I suppose.'

' Yes, she's personal secretary to a tycoon. But she'll be here at weekends.'

Her brother fetched her empty coffee-cup. ' More?' he asked. ' No? Well, I will, if you don't mind.' He set down her cup, refilled his own, then said matter-of-factly, ' One imagined it would be a set-up like this. It's all quite unsatisfactory. You'd better come and stay with me for a bit.'

' *What?*'

' That's why I brought the car instead of coming by train. We'll just load you aboard—'

' But good gracious, Arnold—I don't want to—'

' Pack a few things. Or better still, let me do it. Which is your room?'

' No, no, I couldn't possibly go—'

' Why not? You'd be far better off in Edinburgh with me. I've got a nice little house in a lane on the north side of the town—you could get out and about quite easily, no flights of stairs to contend with.'

'But Arnold—'

'There's a daily who comes in—she'd get a meal for you. And my students drop in a lot, so you'd have plenty of company.'

'Arnold, really, I—'

'You'd like Edinburgh. There's a lot going on all the time. Not as much as London, of course, but there's countryside on your doorstep—hills and the sea. You might even come and see my dig,' Arnold said, looking pleased.

'Your dig?'

'Yes. A Roman fortress, near Braco in Perthshire. Quite a project, I assure you. Now, which room did you say?'

'Which room what?' she said, baffled.

'Which room is yours? I'd better pack some sweaters and things, because it's cooler up north than in London.'

Lindy made a great effort to regain control of events. 'Arnold,' she said in a clear voice, after taking a deep breath, 'I am not coming to Edinburgh with you.'

'But why not?'

'Why not? Because . . . because it's years since we saw each other and it would be hideously embarrassing. Because we never did have much in common and we have even less now. Because it never entered my head to call on you for help—'

'In a way,' he interrupted, 'that's why I'm here. You know, Lindy, it's all wrong. I can't pretend I understood your motives when you packed up and left—'

'I thought I made that clear in my letter.'

'Not to me.' He sighed. 'Well, let's not go into that now. The point is, Lindy, brother and sister ought not to drift out of touch like that. Especially when there's no reason for it.'

'I had a reason,' she insisted.

'But that was two years ago. As you yourself said, a person can change in two years. I admit I was astonished at the way you just walked out, especially in the circumstances. . . .' He paused, eyed her, and decided not to say whatever else had been in his mind. 'Anyhow, the point is, I'm your brother and I've got a home where you'd be a lot more comfortable than you are here, at least until you're fully mobile again. I'd very much like you to come.'

All her instincts told her to refuse. 'I don't really think it would be a good idea, Arnold.'

He took off his glasses to rub his eyes. Without them he looked less alarming. He glanced up at her. 'Please, Lindy,' he said. 'Don't you understand that I'm trying to say I'm sorry?'

So in the end she agreed, and rang Julia at her office to explain that her brother had come to collect her for a convalescence in the north. She could tell by Julia's voice that she was relieved over the decision; a very busy secretary, Julia simply didn't have the time or the energy to act nursemaid to a chair-bound flatmate. 'Have a good time,' she told Lindy, 'and don't hurry back. I'll send on any correspondence and so forth.'

Two hours later Lindy was in her brother's Ford station-wagon, bowling northwards on the motorway. She had done her own packing with some help from Arnold, then had hobbled painfully downstairs while he went to fetch the car from the underground car park where he had left it. This experience had left her thankful at the idea of not having to do it again until she was fully mobile.

They stopped for lunch at Longborough and for a leisurely dinner in Berwick-on-Tweed. Consequently it was very late when at last they reached the environs of Edinburgh. Lindy was drowsing; all she was conscious of was a ribbon of bright light as they moved swiftly along a wide main street, and then a glimpse of sky and stars and a coastline as they swept down a hilly road. She afterwards discovered that the brightly-lit main street was Princes Street, and that the view she had seen was the coastline of Fife seen from the top of Frederick Street.

But she was only half aware of her surroundings that night, even when the car stopped. Arnold helped her out. Under the shoe of her good foot she felt cobbles. The air was sharply cold, colder than an April night would be in London. Arnold opened a door for her to enter; the little hall was warm, welcoming. There was a scent of freesias from an amateurishly-arranged vase on a dark oak table. Sleepily she glanced about, agreed with alacrity when her brother suggested she would like to go straight to bed, and was carried up a short flight of stairs to a small room, very neat and unpretentious.

'If there's anything you want, just shout,' said Arnold. 'Bathroom straight across the passage. Don't get up in the morning until you feel like it—Mrs Ramsay arrives at ten, so she'll get breakfast for you. Goodnight.'

'Goodnight, Arnold.' Almost in a daze she went through a sketchy routine of removing her make-up and brushing her long hair. She fell into bed. Her last conscious thought was one of gratitude to the kindly Mrs Ramsay who had presumably put a hot water bottle between the sheets before she left at the end of her day's work.

When she woke, it was to the extraordinary notion that she could hear water running—not tap-water, but the burbling of a stream going over stones. She opened her eyes. Above her head a patch of sunlight twinkled on the ceiling—twinkled in the way that sunlight does when it reflects off water.

Sitting up, she looked around her. She saw a squarish room with a window curving out from it in a bow. Rather stiffly she got out of bed, pulled a dressing-gown around her shoulders, and went to look out.

Below her a river flowed—an amber-coloured river flecked with creamy foam caused by the current's tussle with a patch of grey-beige boulders. On one of the boulders a long-tailed black-and-white bird was standing, bobbing its head as it surveyed the world. Over his head there was a spread of boughs, sparsely clad in light green leafage, through which a clear, rather cool yellow light filtered down from the spring sun.

Lindy was taken aback. Little as she knew about the city, she had been certain that Edinburgh was a place of houses and offices and churches and museums: a built-up area, a structure of streets and traffic, like London only smaller. But the view outside her window was like the country; she could imagine herself in Devon or Cornwall except that perhaps the quality of the daylight had a feel of the north.

The wagtail on the stones spread his wings and flew up into the trees. Smiling in pleasure, Lindy hobbled to the dressing table to pin up her hair before washing and dressing. While she was engaged on this, someone tapped on her door.

'Can I come in? Good morning, Miss Gramont.' In came a small round woman in a nylon overall of a blue as brilliant as her round eyes. 'I thought you'd like a cup of tea. How's yourself this morning?'

'Oh, how nice. *Thank* you.' Lindy accepted the tray, smiling over it at the bearer. 'You're Mrs Ramsay?'

'Aye, that's me. Did you sleep well? I left oot some sandwiches and a vacuum jug of coffee, but I see this morn they've no' been touched. You'll be hungry, eh?'

'Well . . . no . . . I never am in the morning. The tea's lovely, though.'

'Well, just you get ready in your ain good time and then come you doon the stairs, and I'll have your breakfast ready.'

'No, really, Mrs Ramsay, I never eat breakfast—'

'Tut-tut, you canna walk aboot with nothing inside you. I'll just make you some porridge and maybe an egg, and that'll see you through until you get a proper meal at lunchtime!'

So saying, Mrs Ramsay bustled off, her grey, neatly-permed hair bobbing with the force of her movements. Lindy grinned at herself in the mirror as she finished the tea. If porridge and an egg was not 'a proper meal', what would lunch prove to be?

15

She took her time about getting ready. There was a great pleasure in the feeling of being unhurried: no appointments to keep, no marketing to do. One of the drawbacks of her career in London was the necessity to be up and about at crack of dawn, to get to Covent Garden for her flowers. She had done it willingly, week in, week out, for love of the work and the fulfilment she found in it, but it could only be enjoyable when she felt completely fit. Sometimes in winter, when she had taken on perhaps too many commitments and was a little under the weather, the need to be up early had seemed a tyranny, scarcely compensated for even by the scent of the massed boxes of carnations, roses, chrysanthemums, violets, early mimosa or jasmine.

Now, for the first time in many months, there was time to sit on the dressing-stool and braid her chestnut hair into Victorian loops over her ears, to blend eyeshadow so that it exactly set off her gold-flecked brown eyes, to try a necklace and then a scarf against the dark green cashmere of her dress, and at last to make her unhurried way downstairs to meet the smell of fresh toast and coffee.

Mrs Ramsay greeted her in the little hall. 'Would you mind eating in the kitchen? I've the cleaner going in the dining room and I'm no' sure there's enough room for you and me *and* the carpet-brush!'

'That's quite all right—I'm perfectly happy to— Oh, how nice!' She had walked into a room that might have come straight out of a folk-museum—a polished steel range with a fire glowing red, a scrubbed deal table, an old-fashioned dresser with open shelves above and a skirt of blue-and-white checked gingham below. From behind the gingham a small tabby cat emerged, surveyed her, yawned, stretched, and then rubbed against her plaster-cast ankle in welcome.

'There now! Meg Merrilies has taken to you! She doesna take to everybody, you know.'

'That's very complimentary.' She stooped to tickle the cat under the chin, and was rewarded with a blissful purr. 'What's her name again?'

'Meg Merrilies. She's a wee gypsy, you see.' As Lindy clearly did not see, Mrs Ramsay kindly explained, 'Meg Merrilies is a gypsy girl in a novel by Sir Walter Scott. A friend of your brother's gave her the name, poor wee soul, because she wandered in one night drenched with the rain, and shivering.'

Despite her contention that she never ate breakfast, Lindy found she did justice to the food Mrs Ramsay had prepared. She intended to go out as soon as she had finished, but by that time the clear sunshine of an hour ago had given place to a grey, steely rain, so that the cosiness of a place by the kitchen range seemed irresistible. She was lingering there, finishing the last of the coffee, the little cat curled in her lap, when she heard the front door open and close.

Meg Merrilies sat up. A voice called, 'Mrs Ramsay, are you there?' The cat launched herself from Lindy's knees with a downward thrust of little claws that would, she felt sure, leave a cluster of little red scratches.

'Hello, Meggie,' said the newcomer in the hall.

Lindy half-rose from her seat. Surely she knew that voice?

Mrs Ramsay had switched off the vacuum cleaner. There was a muffled conversation. Then the kitchen door was pushed further open and a man came in.

'Hello, Lindy,' he said.

And she found herself staring at Robert Blair, the man she had practically left waiting at the church when she ran away from her home in Cambridge two years earlier.

CHAPTER II

She was quite unable to speak. It was as if a ghost from the past had reared up in her path. She felt for the high-backed wooden chair behind her and sank back into it, feeling all the blood drain out of her face at the shock of his arrival.

Rob Blair came up to the fire, his hands held out to the glow to warm them. The cat was weaving round his ankles in ecstasy. He nudged it gently with the toe of his shoe, but his attention was on Lindy.

' How are you?' he inquired. ' Did you have a good journey?'

She still had no voice with which to reply. She moved her head convulsively, and he said, his tone alarmed, ' Are you all right?'

She swallowed hard. ' Yes, thanks. How . . . how are you, Rob?'

' Well enough. I didn't expect you to have arrived yet, otherwise I wouldn't have come like this, unannounced. I just came to leave some flowers.'

' I didn't expect you to be here *at all*,' she countered. ' What are you . . . what are you doing here, Rob?'

' Doing here? I live here.'

' Here?' she echoed, horror-stricken.

' Oh, not in this house. Here in Edinburgh—or at least nearby, in a little village called Cramond.'

' But I thought . . . I mean, the last I knew, you were in Cambridge.'

' Well, you haven't bothered to make any inquiries, have you?' he remarked. ' Arnold could have told you any time you cared to ask. I left Cambridge soon after you—' He broke off, paused, and then resumed with perfect composure. ' I'm in business here.'

' In business?' The last she had known, he was teaching at an agricultural college in Cambridgeshire. She couldn't imagine him as a businessman; somehow he didn't seem the type.

'Yes, a cousin of mine was retiring, giving up work. He had a nursery at Cramond—'

'A *nursery*?'

'A plant nursery,' he said, amused. 'Two acres of glass—stephanotis, carnations, gardenias. And some rare house plants. It's a paying concern.'

That made sense. As a teacher his subject had been horticulture, and he had undoubtedly been good at it— his students won award scholarships for original research on plant-breeding and analysis. She was a little sur- prised that he had given it up, for he had loved the work; but a moment's thought made her realise that a man who has been jilted two weeks before the wedding is quite likely to want to get away from the places and faces associated with such a fiasco.

Lindy blamed herself for what had happened. But even more, she blamed her brother. Arnold and Rob had been very good friends from the time that they had happened to meet at a conference on the conservation of the countryside. Arnold had a lectureship in the univer- sity, Rob taught at a residential college not far from the city; they shared many interests in common. Some- how it became accepted that Lindy and Rob would make a good pair, and because of her habit of believing every- thing her brother said, Lindy had found herself trapped in a situation from which she could not escape without family rows, dissension, and distress.

She was immature; looking back she realised that the idea of being engaged had seemed pleasant—faintly glamorous, exciting in an undemanding fashion. But once the wedding day was fixed all her suppressed doubts seemed to rise up in Lindy, towering over her like phantoms. She became aware that this gentle, com- panionable feeling that she had for Rob was not love. It had no passion in it.

What woke her to her dilemma was Rob himself. One night, as he was kissing her goodbye, he had suddenly pulled her close and brought his mouth down on hers with a force that bruised her.

'I love you so much,' he whispered. His voice had been quite different from any normal tone of his—the voice of a stranger.

How she said goodnight and freed herself, she never could recall. All that remained with her was the sense of panic. In her room that night she had sat for hours on her bed, thinking, thinking . . .

She didn't love Rob. She suddenly understood that. The strength of that kiss had told her—she, Lindy Gramont, had never known what it was to long for someone, to want to be as one with someone.

Somehow she had imagined marriage as a sort of continuation of the engagement—a warm and friendly partnership. That parting kiss from Rob had been like the tearing aside of a curtain. She knew, from that moment, that she could not marry him. She could not think of him as a lover. He was more like a brother to her; she liked him, depended on him, respected him. But she could not make love with him.

She knew now that she should have had the courage to tell him this. They could never have gone back to their former relationship afterwards, but at least she would have retained her self-respect. However, she had been unable to bring herself to face him or to face Arnold. She had scuttled away, leaving a note to say that she was terribly sorry, that she knew it was all her fault, that she couldn't go through with the forthcoming wedding and begged them both to forgive her.

It was symptomatic, perhaps, that she had not written to Rob. She had written to her brother. In a way her relationship with Rob had seemed a secondary thing even though she had been his fiancée. It seemed to her that none of it would have happened if he had not been her brother's friend, a man whom her brother approved of as a suitable match for her.

She never *had* written to Rob. Duty impelled her, once she had found a job in London and had an address to send, to let Arnold know her whereabouts. He had never replied to that brief note. But at Christmas, when she sent a card, he had reciprocated. When he moved from Cambridge to Edinburgh, he had sent his new address. But he had never written a letter, and nor had she. And so she had been quite unaware that Rob Blair was in Edinburgh, still among Arnold's circle of friends.

If she had known, nothing would have persuaded her to come here.

Here she was now, trapped in a tête-à-tête with the man she would have crossed oceans and deserts to avoid. She looked at him, confused and unhappy: to her consternation he seemed relatively unperturbed.

He was a tall man—not as tall as Arnold, who always seemed to tower over everyone, but long-limbed, erect, with an easy bearing that came from physical fitness. He had always been an outdoor type—a keen walker, a climber, a field botanist who knew every inch of the countryside around the college where he taught. He was, if anything, more deeply tanned than before, and she thought he seemed thinner—but it suited him. He still wore his dark hair very short compared with present-day fashions, but that too suited him, trimming away from the face any extraneous lines so that the wide, thin lips and the straight, rather Roman nose were given prominence.

She said with hesitation, 'Did you . . . Did Arnold tell you he was bringing me here?'

He nodded. 'Of course.'

'He never mentioned you to me,' she said painfully.

'Why should he? All that is in the past.'

'It doesn't seem so to me,' she replied, embarrassment and misery fighting for the upper hand. 'I simply don't know what to say to you.'

'Why say anything, other than hello? I'm willing to let bygones be bygones if you are, Lindy, and start again as if we'd only just met.'

'I don't see how that's possible . . .'

'Why not? Nobody here in Edinburgh knows we

ever met before. Two years have gone by in which we've each been leading our separate lives. We *are* strangers, in that we've both changed—you especially, Lindy.'

'I have? In what way?'

He smiled, a faint movement of the long quiet mouth. 'It's hard to say. You're still a very pretty girl, still have a skin like jasmine petals . . . But you're not shy any more.'

'I feel shy at this moment.'

'No. Embarrassed perhaps. Not shy. You've outgrown it.'

'I hope I'll outgrow the embarrassment too,' she said, rather more crisply than she intended. She was beginning to feel a faint anger. Arnold should have warned her; how dared he let her walk into a situation like this!

'Would you like some coffee?' she inquired.

'No, thank you. I've an appointment in St Andrew's Square in twenty minutes. I didn't expect to find you here this early—Arnold said he thought he'd stay overnight and drive you back today, so I intended to leave some flowers for Mrs Ramsay to put in your room. You were always fond of flowers.'

'I still am.' She was about to explain that they were how she earned her living, but that might mean extending the conversation more than either of them wanted. 'Thank you for the thought,' she said. 'Shall I give Arnold any message?'

'No, thanks, I expect I'll be seeing him. So long, Lindy.'

'So long, Rob.'

And then he was gone, and she sat back, shivering despite the warmth of the fire, exhausted by the encounter.

A little later Mrs Ramsay came in. 'Now, Miss Gramont, I've finished tidying down here. I'm away up the stairs to do the bedrooms. Before I go up, is there anything I can get you?'

'No, thank you.' And then, as the other woman turned to the broom cupboard, she asked, 'Does Mr Blair come here often?'

'Indeed he does. He and your brother are great friends. It was him that named the cat Meg Merrilies, him being a Scot and knowing all the Waverley novels, you see. Oh yes, often here, is Mr Blair.'

Mrs Ramsay looked as if she might stay for a long chat, but Lindy was silent. She knew her expression was cold and vexed, but she made no effort to soften it, and after a hesitant moment Mrs Ramsay collected dusters and polishes and went away.

Lindy had felt the beginnings of anger before. Now it swept over her. How *dared* he! Her brother's high-handed behaviour was beyond anything that could be borne! Not a word had he said—not a word about Rob. If she had asked, would he have admitted that the man she had run away from was a constant visitor to his house?

In fairness she had to admit that he probably would have; Arnold wasn't a liar. But he had known very well that she wouldn't inquire after Rob. That was the very last name that was likely to pass her lips.

Of course, if she had been quick-witted enough or if her memory had been functioning correctly, she would have recalled that Edinburgh was Rob's birthplace. What more likely than he would come back here? Yet it hadn't occurred to her. It had seemed quite natural that her brother should be here in Edinburgh; that had not caused the slightest query in her mind because Edinburgh University had a keen Department of Archaeology taking a special interest in Roman and post-Roman antiquities—which was Arnold's speciality. If she thought of it at all, however, she would have regarded Rob's coming here as unlikely, because she had thought of him as continuing in teaching; and Edinburgh University did not have a department for any of the agricultural sciences.

It simply hadn't occurred to her that Rob would leave

teaching. In fact, it simply hadn't occurred to her that Rob would continue to have an existence just as she herself had: somehow, by banishing him from her own life, she had made it seem as if he had disappeared for ever.

But that simply wasn't so. Rob still existed, still continued to be a friend of her brother's: and Arnold still continued to think that Rob would make a good brother-in-law.

That was the only explanation. In his domineering way, Arnold had decided that now was the time to bring the two of them together again.

Well, she would show him! She wasn't a marionette, to be manipulated by his strong and clever fingers. She was a person in her own right, with two years of hard work and success to prove it. She would go back to London, now, this very minute, as a demonstration of her independence.

She rose with clumsy haste and began the climb up the short flight of stairs of the cottage. Mrs Ramsay, hearing her, came out to the landing with a duster in her hand.

' Don't you come up if there's something I can bring down to you, Miss Gramont.'

' No, thank you, Mrs Ramsay. I'm coming up to pack.'

' To pack? Michty me, what for?'

' To go back to London.'

' But you only just got here, Miss Gramont'l.'

' And now I'm going straight back again.' Lindy had completed the climb and now went into her bedroom. Mrs Ramsay, greatly agitated, followed her.

' Miss Gramont, your brother will be very surprised! He telt me to look after you as much as I could and make you a nice lunch, and—'

' It won't do my brother any harm to be surprised,' said Lindy.

' Miss Gramont . . . is it because of me?'

' You?' Lindy was astounded at the question.

'Well, I mean, is it because ye dinna tak' to me? If I've been a nuisance to you with my blether . . .' The more perturbed Mrs Ramsay grew, the more pronounced her Scots accent became. Lindy was beginning to find her hard to follow.

'It's nothing to do with you,' she said calmly. 'It's a private matter. Now if you don't mind, I'd like to get on with my packing.'

The other woman nodded silently and withdrew. Lindy put her suitcase on the neatly made bed, opened it, and began to put back the few items she had already taken out.

She glanced out of the window. Rain was falling steadily past the boughs of the trees on the opposite bank of the river. She would have to call a taxi to get her to the station. Was there a train at this hour? She glanced at her watch: five minutes past midday. Surely there would be a London train at lunchtime or soon after.

Money. She looked in her handbag. She had come away at such short notice that she had almost no money with her, but she could cash a cheque at any bank on production of her cheque card. That meant she would have to get the taxi to take her to a bank so that she would have money to pay for the train ticket. And she must ask the taxi to wait for her outside the bank.

She was so deep in this complex train of thought that she didn't hear the sounds downstairs nor Mrs Ramsay descending. But as she was snapping shut the locks on her case, the room door opened.

'Mrs Ramsay tells me you're leaving,' said Arnold. She turned. 'Yes. On the next available train.'

'May one ask why?'

'Didn't Mrs Ramsay tell you that too?'

'Don't be childish, Lindy. Mrs Ramsay only knows what you told her. What's the meaning of all this?'

'You're the one who should be answering that question,' she flared. 'How dare you bring me here to this house when you knew very well that Rob Blair walked in and out of it as if he lived here?'

Arnold's square face went stiff with concern. 'So that's it,' he said, an unaccustomed uncertainty coming into his voice. 'You've seen him?'

'I talked to him. He strolled in about an hour ago. It was the most hideously embarrassing moment in my life.'

'Couldn't have been much fun for Rob, either. I wasn't supposed to be back until this evening.'

'But he at least knew I was coming. I, on the other hand, was totally unprepared. Which was what you intended,' she added, her eyes resting on him in icy accusation.

'Oh, now look here, Lindy, you've no grounds for saying that—'

'Do you deny that you avoided telling me Rob was here in Edinburgh and that you saw him frequently?'

'I was going to tell you—as soon as you asked after him.'

'You must surely have known I would never mention Rob Blair.'

'I don't see why not. He doesn't avoid mentioning you. But then,' Arnold pointed out, ' *he* has nothing to be ashamed of where you're concerned.'

'Meaning that I have. All right, I admit it. I behaved very badly. My only excuse is that I was overcome with panic.'

'Panic doesn't last for ever, my dear girl. Shouldn't you at least have written to him by this time, explaining and apologising?'

'I asked you to apologise in the letter I left,' she protested.

'But you didn't explain. Don't you feel you owed him an explanation—and still do?'

'Is that why you brought me here?' she demanded. 'To make me explain to Rob why I ran away? Can't you face the fact that you practically railroaded me into a marriage that I didn't want, simply because you thought any friend of yours would make an ideal husband?'

Arnold was shocked—she could see it by the way his head jerked up. But he said with great calmness, 'My dear girl, I brought you here because you had had an accident that made you unfit to be left cooped up at the top of an inconvenient old house in town. After all, I do feel some responsibility for you—'

'No one asked you to be responsible for me—'

'And I don't think,' he went on, overriding her angry interjection, 'that you have any idea how poorly you looked. A fall like that is quite a shock both physically and mentally, and you were so pale and tired—'

'Oh, spare me the hearts and flowers!' Lindy cried. 'The truth of the matter is, you thought two years ago that I ought to marry Rob Blair, you still think so now, and you brought me here intending to see that it actually happens this time!'

Her brother studied her through his heavy glasses. 'You've grown very vain over the years I haven't seen you,' he remarked. 'You didn't use to have such a high opinion of yourself.' He paused, and then said, giving weight to the words, 'What makes you think that Rob Blair wants you now?'

That stopped her short. She made a sound that was almost a gasp.

'Do you really imagine that you're so irresistible?' Arnold went on cruelly. 'All you have to do is re-appear, and he'll fall at your feet—is that it? It's quite likely he doesn't particularly care for you, either, you know.'

'But . . . but . . . I just thought . . . I mean, he hasn't married anyone else.'

'What makes you think so? You haven't seen or heard of him for over two years.'

'You mean he is married?'

'As a matter of fact, no. But neither are you, so that doesn't prove anything.' Arnold smiled with some satisfaction. 'One of your faults always was that you lacked logic, Lindy. You always preferred intuition to reasoned argument—and in that respect you certainly haven't changed. If you'll just look at the facts calmly, you'll see you've let yourself be run away with by your own emotions—the chief of which seem to be alarm and embarrassment.'

Lindy sat down on the side of the bed, feeling—as so often in the past—that Arnold was running rings round her. 'I *am* alarmed and embarrassed,' she admitted. 'I feel I've got reason to be.'

'Nonsense. Look at the facts, I told you. You had an accident. I was informed. I brought you here for a little rest while your ankle heals. I am at present living and working in Edinburgh—'

'Where it just so happens that my ex-fiancé is living and working,' she took it up.

'It doesn't "just so happen". I'm here because Rob took the trouble to let me know the lectureship in the Archaeology Department was about to fall vacant. I was able—'

'Rob did that? He helped you—?'

'Yes, he did. What did you imagine? That we'd become sworn enemies because you treated him badly?'

'No . . . o,' she said, trying to sort it out in her mind. She was so used to the idea that Arnold controlled every set of circumstances that the idea of his being helped by someone else was almost beyond her. 'Rob was here before you?'

'Why, yes. It's his home town—his family are still scattered about here. After you . . .' he hesitated . . . 'after you left Cambridge, he wanted to make a change and the opportunity came up—so he took it. Apparently he'd always wanted to experiment with new ideas for raising tender plants. It was a struggle at first, but now it's beginning to pay off.'

'I'm glad.'

'That's handsome of you,' he replied sardonically. 'What it amounts to is that you wish him well but you'll run a mile rather than be polite to him.'

'That's not true—'

'What are you doing now? You're packing to leave.'

'Yes, but—I just think it would be less embarrassing for both of us.'

'Was Rob embarrassed when you spoke to him?'

'Well, no . . . Surprised, rather.'

'I've explained about that. He didn't expect you to be here till this evening.'

'But that's just my point, Arnold. He knew I was coming. You discussed it with him.'

'That was purely accidental. He often drops in, and he happened along while I was ringing St George's Hospital the day before yesterday, after I got that postcard. Naturally when I hung up, I told him—and as the hospital Sister I spoke to said they weren't very happy about your flat four storeys up, it seemed equally natural to chat about it. The upshot was, I came to fetch you.'

'But you said he often spoke about me.'

'I said, if my memory serves me right, that he doesn't avoid mentioning you. That's what I'm trying to convey to you—he treats it as something that's over and done with. I don't see why you can't do the same.'

'That's what he said,' she murmured. 'I'm willing to let bygones be bygones . . .'

'There you are, then.' He shrugged. 'Come on, little sister. You're not nearly as fit as you think you are, and four hundred miles each way in two days is a bit much. Besides, look at the weather.'

She followed his glance. The sky was groaning with rain clouds.

'I came home on purpose to have lunch with you,' Arnold urged. 'Mrs Ramsay has two fresh salmon steaks to grill for us.'

'Do you think I'll give in to blandishments like that?' she countered, beginning to laugh.

'I find them easier to offer than the real reason—which is that this two-year separation has ended and we ought not to let it begin again. After all, we are brother and sister, Lindy.'

'Big brother and little sister.'

'Very well, if it bothers you—I promise not to interfere in your life again. I won't even urge you to eat the salmon.'

'Why? Because you think you could eat it all yourself?'

'That's better!' Smiling, he took her case from her and put it on the floor. 'Mrs Ramsay will unpack all that again. Come on down and have a celebratory sherry.'

Without a doubt, there was a great deal of pleasure to be got out of living in her brother's house and being cosseted by Mrs Ramsay. For about a week almost nothing happened; she slept late, ate what Mrs Ramsay put in front of her, was taken out for a drive when the sun shone and discovered that both the hills and the sea were only minutes away. The long hours indoors passed in reading, sewing, and rearranging the flowers which Mrs Ramsay mishandled every time she put them in a vase. One or two people came to call, but not Rob, much to her relief. Mostly they were students either taking archaeology or helping with the dig at Braco.

By the Sunday, she was feeling much better. Her ankle had ceased to ache which, she hoped, meant that it was mending. The sunshine of late April was sparkling on the river that ran behind the cottage—she had discovered that it was called the Water of Leith, and had spent many a dreamy hour watching the anglers casting their patient rods into its splashing brown current.

'How about a little run out to Gullane?' Arnold suggested. 'There's rather a good hotel out there—we could get a very passable lunch and take a look at the sea.'

'Wouldn't you rather go and look at your dig?'

'Not today. If I'm going to dig, I usually go on the Friday evening and spend all Saturday and Sunday . . . Besides, there might be some people at Gullane—friends of mine—we often foregather there on a Sunday.'

Since he quite clearly wanted to go but didn't want

to leave her alone in the house, Lindy agreed that this was a lovely day for a drive to the coast. He loaded her into the Ford estate-car, went back for a coat 'because it can be fresh on that shore', and they were off.

When they reached it, Gullane proved to be a handsome little town, very neat, dominated by its golf links which spread like a green mantle over the dunes next the beach. They sat for a while on a bench watching the players, listening to the purring, twittering notes of the dunlins scampering on the sand, enjoying the sun.

But she could sense her brother's restlessness. Out of politeness, because he knew she needed fresh air and sunshine yet was not able to stroll about on her own, he stayed where he was. But she knew he wanted to move on to the hotel where he could meet his friends.

So after a short time she said, 'Is it too early yet to start thinking about lunch?'

'Not a bit. We could have a drink first—there's rather a nice cocktail lounge.' He jumped up eagerly, heading for the car, then remembered she couldn't walk so fast. Duty-bound, he slowed his step, helped her into the Ford, and settled her comfortably. She smiled to herself; considering that looking after people didn't come naturally to him, he was doing it rather well.

The Hundergate Hotel stood on the outskirts of the little town, down a driveway between windswept meadows but sheltered from the onshore winds by a coppice of birch and rowan. The building gleamed with fresh white paint; the entrance was canopied in spick-and-span blue canvas. Lindy was suddenly glad that, in view of the fact that they would be meeting people, she had taken some care over her appearance, for the place had elegance.

Now that the rest and comfort of the past week were taking effect, she had regained some colour—although her skin was naturally pale. Still, looking in the mirror that morning, she'd noted with forgivable satisfaction that her lips were a healthy pink and her brown eyes had a shine. She had spent the requisite ten minutes on brushing her long mane of hair before piling it high on her head, with little corkscrew spirals softening the line at her temples.

Her wardrobe had caused her some concern. Packing in haste, and bringing only one large case and one small, she had had to strike a compromise between warm clothing for the colder north and easy-care fabrics for convenience. She had really been limited to a skirt and sweater; but the skirt was oatmeal tweed, the sweater was a bulky-knit in a honey tone that matched the flecks in her eyes, and she had given the outfit a final note of chic with a Dior neckscarf of silk, a little square of beige and blue and green like a pheasant's feather.

The whole effect was marred, of course, by the plaster cast on her foot. But as she moved slowly through the hotel's reception lounge to the cocktail bar, she knew from the admiring glances that none of the men noticed that.

The cocktail bar was at the back of the building, in what amounted to a big glassed-in verandah looking out to sea. The place was crowded, but a welcoming cry went up from a corner as they appeared.

'Arnold! How nice! So here you are—come on, sit down!' A place was cleared for them on the blue-leather bench that ran the length of the wall. Tables were pushed aside to make room.

There were about eight people of varying ages, some old but mostly young—student age or thereabouts. Introductions were effected. Most of her new acquaintances said they had heard about Lindy's visit, and how was the ankle, and was she liking Scotland?

Lindy laughed, 'You can hardly expect me to say anything about Scotland when my knowledge of it, so far, consists of Arnold's little house and a few drives in a car!'

'He's treating you well, is he?'

'Obviously he's not, or he would have got the poor lass a drink!'

'True enough! What are you having, Lindy?'

32

She decided to settle for a sherry. Three eager young men rushed off to fetch it. An older man chatted to her or a moment; she gathered he was on the Faculty of Science at the University, but never did find out in what capacity, because at that moment Rob Blair came in.

The same chorus of welcome went up. Obviously he was one of the group. He nodded pleasantly at Lindy, then was cornered by an eager boy with flaming red hair, who began with, 'Robbie, I need your advice. Which is the quickest route up Ben Lomond from Aberfoyle? I've got some Norwegians coming for a weekend and I want to show them a few views . . .'

The rest of the conversation was lost to her. She remembered now that Rob had always been interested in mountains, that from time to time while he was in Cambridge he would disappear—a weekend in the Peak District, ten days in the Juras. She should have known then that he meant too little to her—because, looking back, she realised she'd had never worried about him on those climbing expeditions.

She glanced about for Arnold, but he was deep in talk at the far end of the bench, with a tiny, pretty girl in dark red. Her head was bent so that Lindy couldn't see her face properly; she could make out a high cheek-bone, a small determined chin, and one perfectly-formed ear revealed by a cap of ash-blonde hair worn close against the nape of the neck but in a full soft fringe over the forehead.

Something in the way Arnold was attending to her made Lindy wonder, for one wild moment, if it was for this girl's company that he had been so eager. Then she laughed at herself: her brother had reached the ripe old age of thirty-four without being attracted to anything more feminine than the caryatid from some old Greek temple. It wasn't likely that he'd suddenly fall for anyone so totally human and contemporary as this pretty little flaxen-poll.

Her drink was brought. She found herself drawn into an argument about theatre-in-the-round versus the picture-frame stage.

'I don't know why you imagine I know anything about it—' she began when appealed to.

'Ah, but you're from London, where all the bright lights are! The theatre capital of the world.'

'Oh, don't be absurd, Hamish, New York is the theatre capital of the world—'

'That shows how much you know about it. New York can only produce modern pieces. It has no *background*, no—'

'Marion, you've been to New York. What do you think?'

The girl talking to Arnold looked up. 'Think about what?' she inquired.

'About the New York stage.'

'What makes you think I know anything about the New York stage, John, for goodness' sake?'

'Well, you've been there.'

'But only to take part in a music festival. I spent all my time on the concert platform, in the rehearsal room, or asleep from exhaustion in my hotel.'

'You must have gone to the theatre at least once, surely,' John protested.

'No, not once. I went to the opera, if that counts?'

John shrugged and went back to his argument. Lindy, who knew little or nothing about theatre technique, leaned across the glass-and-wrought-iron table to attract Marion's attention.

'Did you say you went to New York for some musical event?'

'Yes, the New York Contemporary Music Festival.'

'You took part?'

Marion nodded. 'I have a degree in music—graduated last year. The piano's my instrument.'

'Oh, how marvellous! Are you going to make it your career?'

'Only as a teacher,' the other girl said. There was a muted bitterness in her voice, masked behind a pretended insouciance. 'I thought I might be a concert

ianist, but the New York Festival taught me different
—I didn't even come among the runners-up in the piano
wards.'

'Oh, I see . . . it was that kind of festival,' Lindy
aid lamely. 'One where they have a sort of contest.
Not like the one you have here in Edinburgh?'

'*Our* Festival's a thing on its own,' said Rob's voice.
He had drifted up to their table, whether on purpose or
y accident she couldn't tell. 'This year Marion's going
o light up the Fringe for us.'

'Light up the Fringe?' she echoed, laughing at the
picture.

'Set it in a blaze. You know the Fringe is all the
unofficial stuff that goes on in Edinburgh during the three
weeks of the official Festival. While the Royal Shake-
speare Company is solemnly playing out "Macbeth" in
the King's Theatre, some irreverent group will be par-
odying it in a show called "MacBreath" in a church
hall in St Vincent Street.'

'Why is it called the Fringe?' Lindy inquired.

'Oh, I think it's from a phrase that used to be in
vogue to describe the folk who got carried away by ballet
and opera—"the lunatic fringe". Also, of course, the
people who fill all the church halls and school gyms with
activity during the Festival *are* on the fringe of the official
programme.'

'Are you going to do something lunatic on the
Fringe?' Lindy asked Marion in a teasing tone.

A certain iciness seemed to tinge the dark blue of
Marion's eyes. 'Certainly not. I'm a serious musician.'

'Lindy didn't mean it that way,' Arnold soothed.
'Don't forget she's never even seen a Festival—she
hasn't the remotest idea of the range of happenings.'

'Yes, I'm sorry, I didn't mean to be clumsy,' Lindy
said. 'Do tell me what you're going to do.'

'It isn't settled yet. It's only the beginning of May
now—four months to go till the Festival. A lot depends
on Lorenz.'

'Who's Lorenz?'

35

' You may well ask,' piped up one of the young male students at the far end of the bench, having by some trick of acoustics caught this question. ' He's the bane of our lives, isn't he, fellows? All the girls are crazy about him. Makes life difficult for the rest of us!'

' What nonsense,' Marion said in amusement.

But then her glance travelled beyond Lindy, and her expression changed. Lindy looked over her shoulder to see a man coming into the cocktail bar. He was tall, with rather long tawny hair framing a long face lit by the liveliest, brightest grey-green eyes Lindy had ever seen.

She knew, without being told, that this was Lorenz. Some indefinite difference in him told her he was a foreigner. He came up to their table, smiled at them all, took one of Marion's hands and raised it to his lips.

' Am I late?' he inquired. ' I seem to be the last.'

' Last but not least,' Marion murmured. Something about her had altered from the moment he appeared. She seemed to have gained a soft radiance. ' Of course you're not late, darling—lunch is ordered for half past one.'

' Schön,' he said. ' It is good to be away from the problems. The travel arrangements for the Kiev State Choir once again must be altered—they will now be in South America just before the Festival, instead of in Kiev.'

' Oh, poor Lorenz!'

' Are you connected with the Kiev State Choir?' Lindy said in surprise. His accent had not struck her as Russian.

For the first time he brought his glance to rest on her. He looked almost surprised, as if he hadn't expected to see anyone like her—she bore the stamp of London in her clothes, her make-up, her hair-style. He smiled a sudden welcome.

She found herself strangely breathless under that smile. She became aware of a strange thumping in her breast— her own heart, whose beat was usually so tranquil that she was unaware of it.

36

'Let me introduce Lorenz Hemer—he's on the staff of the Festival Organisation, does the travel arrangements for all the foreign orchestras and so forth. My sister Lindy, Lorenz.'

'So,' he said, 'your sister?' He took Lindy's hand and kissed it. 'It gives me pleasure,' he said.

It gives me pleasure. She herself could have used those words as she felt his lips touch the back of her wrist. She was conscious of a strange thrill of delight, new to her, warm and glowing within her.

And she was conscious, too, that Marion had gone tense with anger.

CHAPTER III

Lindy reflected afterwards that virtue really is its own reward. She had gone out with Arnold that morning simply to please him, because he seemed keen to go. As a result, she had met Lorenz.

The meal they shared was excellent. The hotel restaurant seemed to know them all well; an L-shaped group of tables had been reserved for them at which a portly old waiter gave them his undivided attention. Coffee was served in the lounge. Although Lorenz had been some distance away during lunch, Lindy saw with gratification that he took pains to be beside her as they settled themselves for coffee.

'You have just come to Edinburgh?' he asked.

'I've been here a week.'

'So long, and I have not met you? What a waste!' He pulled a face, his mobile mouth twisting. 'And you have had a skiing accident with the foot, I take it.'

'Nothing so glamorous. I fell off a ladder.'

'Really? It is more *unusual* than a ski accident, at this time of year,' he chuckled. 'You know, at the airports and stations, from Christmas until the end of April, you see people hobbling home from my country with broken bones.'

'Your country—are you Swiss?'

'Austrian. From Vienna, the city of waltzes and romance—at least, that is where I was trained. I spent most of my boyhood there. I was born in Carinthia, which you have never heard of, but which borders on Italy and Yugoslavia. Very beautiful, you know—great mountains and lakes. Do you know the highest mountain in Austria is in Carinthia—the Gross Glockner?'

'I never heard of that either,' Lindy bantered. 'And what did you train for—skiing?'

'In Vienna? You are joking. In Vienna it is either music or horses—and I am afraid of horses. No, I was a pianist.'

'Like Marion?'

Lorenz turned his head, but Marion appeared not to have heard the mention of her name. She was talking earnestly to Rob.

'Better than Marion,' he replied calmly. 'I had a career on the concert platform that lasted three or four years. Marion is never going to make it, you know. Her hands are too small—she can barely span an octave.'

Lindy felt a stab of pity. 'That's sad. She seems terribly keen. Isn't it possible to be a good pianist if one's hand is small?'

'Oh yes, good. But not good enough when there are so many who are better—who are *the best*. I realised this myself. I play well. I think even that I play very well. But what is that compared with Claudio Arrau, with Ashkenazy, with Barenboim? So I came to terms with it. I realised that I was never going to be *great*, and decided to do something else, something that would keep me in the world of music. So here I am, helping to organise the Edinburgh Festival—and I am very glad, because it allowed me to meet you.'

She met his admiring gaze. 'That's sheer flattery!'

'I am not quite sure whether that means in English it is good or it is bad. But I see by your expression that you are pleased, and that is all that matters.'

She couldn't think of anything to say in reply to that.

Shortly afterwards the party began to split up. Some of the men had an engagement to play golf later in the afternoon, so would be staying. Others had to get back to Edinburgh. A rearrangement of travelling facilities became necessary. Arnold offered to take Hamish south to Berwick: 'Do you mind going on to Berwick before we go home, Lindy?'

'Oh, that will not be necessary,' Lorenz said. 'I can take Lindy in my car.' He looked at her for agreement; she nodded.

'Then I'll come with you,' Marion said. 'I want to get home to hear the Stravinsky on the radio.'

'Very well,' said Lorenz, although Lindy thought he was not very pleased.

They wandered out on to the gravel forecourt where the cars were parked, sorted themselves out, and packed themselves in. It was now three o'clock, with the sun still warm in a sky of eggshell blue. As they passed the golf course they could see the foursomes, bright in their anoraks and windcheaters, moving like purposeful birds on the greens.

'This is a game I have never played,' Lorenz remarked. 'I don't understand its fascination—but then there is a great deal I don't understand about the British. This cricket, for instance.'

'Afraid of horses, don't like golf, can't understand cricket,' Lindy teased. 'You must do *something* besides plan itineraries for travelling musicians.'

'He plays the piano,' said Marion.

'So he was telling me.'

'He plays well,' Marion insisted, almost possessively.

'He told me that too. But I meant,' Lindy went on, anxious to keep the peace, 'what do you do for fun, Lorenz?'

'Oh, for fun, I like to dance and go to parties, and I would swim if only the sea got warm enough here, and when I can I sometimes go climbing.'

'That's one of your hobbies too? Rob's a climber.'

'Rob . . . he is your brother's friend, yes? Sometimes I don't always remember who is who.'

'But I thought you knew them all very well . . .?'

'Oh no, I only have met them quite recently.'

'*I* introduced him,' Marion put in. 'He knew hardly anyone, so—'

'Yes, it was very kind of you,' Lorenz said. 'I am very grateful.' He concentrated for a moment on passing a long-distance lorry, then repeated, with a glance out of the corner of his eye at Lindy, 'Ve-ery grateful.'

At the road junction by Aberlady he decided to go inland: 'Too dull, all those power-stations and so forth all along the coast. We shall go south instead.'

'So that is good. You will be in plenty of time for
'But, Lorenz, that means we'll reach my house first.'
the Stravinsky.'
'But what about Lindy?'
'I will take her home after I drop you off.'
'Oh . . . I thought you'd like to come and listen to
the concert with me . . .'
'I'm sorry, I'm expecting a call from Kiev. I must
be at home to take it.'

There was nothing more to be said. Marion had taken
the passenger seat alongside Lorenz; Lindy was in the
back—'so you can have room for your poor ankle,'
Marion had said—and was glad she couldn't see the other
girl's face.

They sped on in the light Sunday traffic, past Tranent
and Dalkeith, glimpsing at the latter a building which
had all the appearance of a palace. Soon they were in
the southern suburbs of Edinburgh; Lorenz slowed to
the permitted speed and turned off to the left, into a
terrace of very tall and rather imposing flats with rows
of brass bell-pulls at the entrance.

Marion got out. She hesitated. 'Wouldn't you like
to come in for a cup of tea?' she offered, then added:
'Both of you?'

'I don't have time,' said Lorenz, 'but perhaps
Lindy—?'

Marion managed not to look taken aback at this. 'It's
three floors up,' she murmured. 'Perhaps it would be
too much for you, Lindy?'

'I think it would, just at present. Thanks very much,
though, Marion. I'll take you up on it some other time
if I may.'

'I'll look forward to it.' It didn't really sound as if
she would. 'Goodbye for the present, then. Goodbye,
Lorenz.'

'Goodbye, Marion, see you soon.' He had got out of
the car to escort her to the door. Now he came back
quickly as she walked on into the hallway, and said to
Lindy: 'Come and sit in the front with me.'

'Oh, it's hardly worth the trouble, Lorenz——'

'To me it is. You want me to sit with my head twisted round to talk to you when I should be looking at the road?'

'No, no, of course not.'

'Come, then.' He helped her out and then into the front passenger seat; that done, he walked round to his own side. As he did so Lindy glanced past him to the doorway of the building. She caught a flicker of movement—Marion, standing back in the shadows, watching them drive away.

Lorenz chose a road that went in a great sweeping curve through an area of green lawns across which a fine modern building sparkled in the evening sunlight. Later she was to learn that this was the new part of the University, and that this expanse of green was known as The Meadows. At a strange little lane, almost like a mews, that ran alongside the approach to the sparkling modern buildings, Lorenz drew to a standstill.

'Why are we stopping?'

'Because if I go on without stopping we shall be home in a few minutes, and I don't want to part from you yet.'

'And your telephone call from Kiev?'

'Let them call again.' He put his arm round her, drew her close, with his other hand turned her face towards him, and was about to kiss her—but she turned away.

'And Marion?' she said.

'What about Marion?'

'I don't know. You must tell me. It's clear there's something to tell.'

'I assure you, nothing!'

She looked into those eager grey-green eyes, and was reassured. Even though Marion might feel she had some claim, on Lorenz's side there was no sense of obligation. 'How long have you known her?'

'Only since I came to Edinburgh in January. We met at a musical evening sponsored by the University.'

'She said something about a programme or an event

in the Festival?'

'Oh yes, she wants to arrange a recital of modern music and asked me to help get some unpublished pieces . . . I have quite a few friends who are composers for the piano.' He moved irritably. 'Why do we discuss Marion?'

'I wanted to know what she means to you.'

'You are jealous?' He was delighted. 'But that is wonderful! It means—'

'It means you have a very good imagination! I'm not jealous. I just don't like misunderstandings.' She paused, remembering that long and mishandled relationship with Rob, most of which had been her fault because she'd never had the courage to analyse her feelings. 'I felt a . . . an atmosphere between you and Marion. I just wanted to know what caused it.'

He spread his hands. 'Who can tell? She is not easy to understand—she is like the violet in the poem —you know it?'

She shook her head.

> ' "*Ein Veilchen auf der Wiese stand*
> *Gebückt in sich und unbekannt . . .*"'

'That means a violet grew in the meadow, Bent in upon itself and unknown . . . No, you would not say "bent in upon itself". It means . . . I don't know . . .'

'Reticent? Withdrawn?'

'Something like that. Marion is "*gebückt in sich*" —she looks inward to herself and does not explain herself easily to others. She has very strong feelings, I think.'

'I think so too,' Lindy sighed.

Lorenz was about to take her in his arms again, but footsteps sounded on the cobbled lane behind them; a solid-looking citizen in a grey overcoat appeared, intent on getting his car out of the mews garage—so as to go to church. With a grimace of exasperation Lorenz switched on the engine of his Rover, backed out, and slowly began to make his way towards the centre of the city.

'Come and have dinner with me this evening, Lindy.'

'No, thank you. Arnold is expecting me to have dinner with him at home.'

'Then invite me to have dinner with you.'

'No, you must stay at home for your phone call from Kiev.'

'Oh, devil take the phone call from Kiev! Lindy, I want to see you this evening.'

'No, Lorenz. Please. I'd rather not.'

'But why not? *Mein Liebling*, why not?'

She felt like saying, 'Because I've had enough for today. Because my pulse is racing and my mind's in a whirl, and I can't forget that glimpse of Marion in the hallway, watching us drive off.' But all she said was, 'Please, Lorenz. There's always tomorrow and the day after that.'

Like a small boy who has tried his best to coax a favour but knows he has failed, Lorenz pushed out his lower lip. Then he gave her a brilliant smile. 'Tomorrow and the day after, however! That's a promise?'

'Yes,' she agreed, laughing, 'it's a promise.'

As he set her down at the door of the little house in Dean Bank Lane, he kissed her lightly on the lips. She shivered under his kiss, and for a moment his hands closed fiercely on her shoulders. But he didn't kiss her again.

'Goodbye, my love, until tomorrow,' he whispered, and was gone.

Although Arnold had gone five miles further on to North Berwick before turning for home, he was already indoors. He looked with curiosity at Lindy as she came in, but said nothing except, 'Enjoy the day?'

'Oh, *yes*, Arnold, it was lovely.'

'Good. Well, plenty of time to go and have a rest before you change for dinner.'

'Change? Oh, Arnold, do I need to bother?' She was suddenly very tired.

'I think it would be nice, don't you? Rob's coming

44

for dinner.'

She stopped in her slow ascent of the stairs. 'I didn't know you'd invited him?'

'No, it was a spur-of-the-moment thing this afternoon.'

'I see.'

'You don't mind?'

'Of course not. This is your house.'

'Off you go, then. Lie down for a bit, put your foot up. I told Rob eight o'clock.'

'Very well.' With wearying, one-at-a-time progress, she reached the top of the stairs and then her room. Thankfully she lay down on her bed, and even more thankfully recalled that she had refused to have Lorenz to dinner. To have had the man who was her past and the man who seemed determined to be her future at the same table would have been too much to contend with.

Yet in the days that followed, it became something she took for granted. Lorenz appeared at some time of the day, every day; it was inevitable that his visits must sometimes coincide with Rob's. For the next seven days or so Lindy was still limited in mobility, so that if Lorenz wanted to see her he more or less had to come to the house. And so it became established—that Lorenz dropped in when he had time, that Rob dropped in if he wanted to talk to Arnold—and the two men met and nothing happened and Lindy got quite used to it.

It began to dawn on her that the awkwardness she had expected between herself and Rob just didn't exist. When he said he was prepared to let bygones be bygones, he really meant just that. Out of her own heightened susceptibility she had imagined that if he came to the house, it was because he wanted to see her; but she soon had to admit that when he came to the house it was to leave flowers for Mrs Ramsay or to talk to Arnold about his dig.

The dig proved to have a lot of importance in the comings and goings around Arnold. He had been given permission to excavate on the site of a huge Roman

45

fortress at the village of Braco in Perthshire.

'I didn't know the Romans ever got to Perthshire,' Lindy protested. 'They stopped at the Roman Wall in Northumberland, surely.'

Arnold frowned at her over the rims of his glasses. 'One really can't understand how you came to be so badly informed, considering that you've had an archaeologist for a brother all your life!'

'Obviously I wasn't paying attention,' she teased. 'All those years I was spending my energy on growing up instead of learning about the Romans. What, actually, were they doing so far north of their territory?'

'Trying to frighten the unruly Picts. One might say that Perthshire was No-Man's-Land in those days—raiding forces dashing south to harass the Romans, legionaries marching north to quell the trouble, but never quite succeeding, or at least not for long. The fortress at Braco housed twenty-six thousand troops.'

'Twenty-six thousand! But that's enormous!'

'Yes, it *is* rather impressive,' he said with smug satisfaction. 'You must come and have a look once your ankle is better.'

That would be quite soon now. She had been to the Out-Patient Department at the Royal Infirmary, where they had looked at the foot, X-rayed the joint, told her it was mending splendidly and said that in another week she could have the plaster off. She reported this jubilantly to Lorenz, who had collected her from Out-Patients and taken her to lunch at a superb little restaurant close to the Usher Hall.

To her surprise, a look of uncertainty swept over his features.

'What's the matter?'

'When you are better, what happens?'

'How do you mean, what happens?'

'Marion McColl tells me Arnold brought you home to mend the ankle. When it is better, do you go back to London?'

She looked down at the snow-white tablecloth; she

46

couldn't help experiencing a little thrill of triumph at the misery in his voice. Rather ashamed of herself, she murmured: 'We could see each other sometimes.'

'Sometimes.'

'You go to London on business, surely?'

'Only when there is a reason. Not often.'

'It isn't far. You could drive down at weekends. Or I could come north.'

'I suppose so,' he sighed. 'Let us not think about it, *Liebchen*. We have at least one more week, perhaps longer.'

She didn't tell him her plan, because she wanted to be sure it was going to work. But she had already begun negotiations to stay in Edinburgh for at least the next six months.

Lindy earned her living by doing floral arrangements on a freelance basis. She had many clients in London who were already demanding to know when she would be back; during her absence a friend, who had trained at the same flower school, had taken over for her.

She would go on with her career in Edinburgh. At present it was the month of May; soon the big influx of tourists would begin, and continue until at least the end of September. During those months hotels, restaurants, conference halls, theatres, prestige offices, boutiques and even private houses would want expert help with their flowers. It only needed a few introductions, a few personal recommendations, and she would be launched into the world of flower arrangement in this northern capital.

She had already written to the two tutors, now good friends, who had given her her education in how to handle flowers; she was waiting to hear if they could give her one or two introductions, both to clients who might use her work and to suppliers in the wholesale flower market. At first, she knew, the commissions would be slow to come in; that didn't matter, she had enough money put by to live through three or four lean weeks.

There were attendant problems, though. She needed a workroom, and a place to live. Accommodation wasn't particularly cheap in the city, nor particularly easy to come by.

When she mentioned this point to Arnold, he looked astounded. 'You can stay here, of course. Why should you look for somewhere else?'

'But, Arnold, I need a place to work with the flowers —to store containers.'

'You can use the old hayloft.'

The old hayloft was over what had once been stabling for a pony to pull the gig, in Victorian times when the little house was built. Arnold used the little stable as a garage, while the loft overhead was full of rubbish accumulated over years by former owners. Lindy found a treasure trove when she started clearing it for her own use: old earthenware marmalade and pickle jars, bread crocks, carriage lamps, hide leather hatboxes, britannia metal candlesticks, teacaddies, an ancient bike with solid tyres, preserving pans with copper bases, a china aspic mould—all of them, except the bike, perfect accessories for flower arranging, the kind of thing you had to scour London for and buy at cut-throat prices.

Mrs Ramsay fell upon them with soda and water, salt and sand, lemon juice, metal polish, and beeswax. Singing happily and loudly—'By cool Siloam's sha-ady rill . . .'—she spent long hours cleaning and polishing, pausing now and again to exclaim, 'My mother had a bread crock just like this,' or 'I mind my grannie making jam in just such a pan!'

Lindy sat beside her, her foot on a rickety stool, listing the finds and noting ideas beside each item. The loft, now that it was cleared, had a businesslike air; she and Mrs Ramsay had got the dustmen to take away the tattered papers and mouse-chewed sacks, and then between them had swept and scrubbed, slapped a coat of white paint on the walls, and installed two trestle tables for working surfaces.

It would be an ideal place for handling flowers. Cool

and airy, with water available downstairs in the garage
—perhaps a little *too* airy, for the frames of the little
mansard windows had warped, letting in draughts of
air off the cool river.

Nevertheless, she had a premonition she would do
good work here. She was prompted to join in with Mrs
Ramsay, who was now singing 'Lead, Kindly Light'
at the pitch of her voice.

'Excellent,' said a voice. 'You're rehearsing for a
recital in the Fringe, I take it?' It was Rob. He came
up the wooden staircase from the garage. 'The Sound
of Music guided me. You sound very happy.'

'I think we *are* very happy,' Lindy returned. For
the first time, she spoke to him totally without restraint;
perhaps the fact that she was busy had something to do
with it. 'How do you like my new premises?'

He stood in the doorway surveying the loft, looking
puzzled.

'Ye didna see it before,' said Mrs Ramsay. 'It's a
thousand per cent better, Mr Blair, I can assure you.
You couldna have invited a body up here in the state it
was.'

'Perhaps I'm being obtuse, but I don't see the necessity for inviting anybody up here . . .'

'Well, that's true. Most of my work will be done
on the clients' premises.'

He was still mystified. 'Clients?'

'Yes, for flower arranging.' She gave him a rapid
résumé of her plans, gesturing about the loft, scarcely
looking at him as she did so.

He commented: 'It seems very ambitious.'

That rather annoyed her. 'It's what I've been doing
in London!'

'I had no idea.'

'No, I suppose not . . . although I thought Arnold
might have mentioned it to you.'

'No.'

'I've told no one else—not even Lorenz.'

'Not even Lorenz?' He had wandered away and

49

was stooping to examine the old leather hatbox. She frowned; had there been something quizzical in his voice? But he went on calmly, 'This is a funny shape, isn't it? I suppose it was for top-hats—'

'It's a bonnet-box, dated about 1870,' she told him, rather pleased that she had been able to identify it from a book in the public library.

'Aye, and look you at these candlesticks,' Mrs Ramsay put in, holding them up proudly. Hard work had restored a partial shine to the pale britannia metal; the rather rough, domestic shape gave them a charm of their own, quite unlike that of the true silver candlesticks of the drawingroom. 'Now these would look bonny with red candles in—'

'No, no, Mrs Ramsay! I shall use them for flowers.'

'They'll have to be gey wee flowers,' she said, peering dubiously into the container.

'Not very big, I suppose, but you can buy cups that will fit into candlesticks so that you can do a goblet arrangement, you know.'

'I can see you're quite an expert,' said Rob.

'You have to be if you earn your living by it.' Once again she was piqued at his reaction. Did he still think of her as the shy, uncertain teenager he had known in Cambridge? Without realising that she was doing it to impress him, she began to describe some of the commissions she'd had in the past, and to wonder where, in these new surroundings, she could find the unusual or expensive flowers that she sometimes needed.

'I'm trying out one or two new plants,' Rob said. 'I wonder if . . .'

'What?'

He took some time before going on, and she guessed that it was because he was uncertain how she would react. At length he said frankly, 'After all, you are in business to use flowers and I am in business to sell them. If you'd care to come and look at the nursery some time, I'd be happy to show you round.'

'Thank you, I'd love to.' She glanced at her watch.

'Tea-time, Mrs Ramsay. Let's go and get something. You'll stay, won't you, Rob?' This invitation was to let him know she quite understood his businesslike attitude.

'Oh, no, I shouldn't want to put you to any trouble—'

'No trouble, Mr Blair—Mr Gramont said he'd be coming home to tea and bringing some of the dig committee—they're going up to Braco this weekend, I'm thinking.'

'In that case . . .'

He helped Lindy to her feet, although by this time she didn't really need help. Mrs Ramsay had already laid a covered tray of cups and saucers in the sitting-room, to which she showed them while she busied herself making tea and cutting cake in the kitchen.

Lindy found herself talking completely without restraint to Rob about flowers. 'Yes, carnations are awfully useful and very popular with the public, although I don't much care for them myself. Which varieties do you grow?'

'I've been working with some of the older varieties, such as Mrs Brotherstone or King of Cloves. I specialise quite a bit on clove-scented carnations—most of the commercially-grown varieties have almost no smell.'

'Yes, isn't it a pity! Do you grow them under glass?'

'Some of them, for a continual supply. But I have quite an area given over to them in the open.' He went on to describe the layout of his nursery, got out a notebook to make sketches. They were deep in discussion when they heard the sound of new arrivals, and a moment later Arnold came in.

'Ah, so there you are, Rob! I tried to ring you at home to ask you to this meeting—but I needn't have bothered, need I?' He smiled from one to the other of them.

'We were talking about flowers,' Lindy explained in haste.

'Of course you were. Good, good. Well, come along in, everyone. Mrs Ramsay, we're here!'

'Aye, I can hear that,' Mrs Ramsay replied, appearing

in a clean nylon overall and with two large earthenware teapots. 'Mind out of my way while I put these down.' Two of the young men following her in relieved her of her burden. One of the girls, without prompting, began to hand round the cake. In the friendly, busy scene Lindy was able to move away unobtrusively from Rob's side. She hadn't liked her brother's look of approval when he came in and found them together; she didn't want him getting any wrong ideas.

Four people had arrived with Arnold; Lindy now discovered, somewhat to her dismay, that one of them was Marion McColl. In the two weeks since that Sunday at Gullane, Lindy had only seen her momentarily, and somehow it had seemed all right to be monopolizing Lorenz when she didn't see Marion.

But now they came face to face. It struck her that Marion seemed a little drawn and tired, that the dark blue eyes seemed bigger and deeper in the heart-shaped face. But the other girl's manner to her was quite polite, even friendly.

Relieved, Lindy joined in the discussion of the week-end's plans—since the weather looked good they would be getting back to work at Braco; there were arguments for and against opening up a new trench.

'Look here, you know as well as I do that until we can raise some money to put some of the trench under cover, it's no use opening a new one,' said Hamish Fordyce, the red-headed student she had already met at Gullane.

'One hopes there will be further allotments of money,' Arnold said, 'in which case—'

'We're not unearthing anything very dramatic, though. Money tends to go to places where there are interesting results.'

'Our results will be interesting. Military equipment—'

'All we've got so far is some broken pots—'

'I can't understand why you didn't begin with the armoury, Arnold,' Rob put in. 'You'd get more chance of finding equipment—'

52

'Not necessarily. When an army packs up and leaves, it tends to take all its equipment from the armoury. One feels that in the officers' quarters, however—'

'From the way you talk about it, it sounds like Chelsea Barracks,' Lindy put in. 'Do you really know where the armoury was, and the officers' quarters?'

Her brother raised his eyes to the ceiling in exasperation. 'Really, Lindy! Do you imagine we're doing all this by a system like water-divining? Of *course* we know where the—'

'Once you get that plaster off your leg, you can come and clamber about on the site,' said Rob. 'I wouldn't advise it until you're able to move quite easily, because the terrain is very uneven, and that coarse grass is devilish slippery after rain.'

'Lindy won't have time to pay us a visit,' Marion ventured. 'She'll be off back to London once she's fit.'

'Och no,' said Mrs Ramsay, coming in at that moment with a replenished teapot. 'Isn't it grand! Miss Gramont's staying on with us after all.'

'Staying on?' There was a clamour of interest from everyone. 'You're going to have a holiday, is that it?'

'No, I'm going to work here. I'm just getting it organized now.'

'That's new,' Marion said. 'And rather sudden—isn't it?'

Under her questioning gaze Lindy felt herself reddening. She said, stammering a little, 'I th . . . thought it would be nice to stay . . . for the Festival, you know. I've never seen the Edinburgh Festival.'

She heard Rob make a little sound—whether it was amusement or irritation, she couldn't tell. At that moment the phone in the hall began to ring. Mrs Ramsay, who was passing, picked it up at once, said, 'Yes, she's here. Just a minute,' then put her head round the sitting-room door.

'It's Mr Hemer,' she announced.

Marion leapt to her feet, almost upsetting her teacup.

'For Miss Gramont,' Mrs Ramsay went on.

More slowly than Marion, because of the plaster cast, Lindy got up. As she made her way to the door she could feel two pairs of eyes upon her.

Rob's, she felt sure, contained only detached curiosity. But in Marion's there was something hotter.

She knew in that moment that, without intending it, she had made an enemy.

CHAPTER IV

At the end of the following week the plaster cast was removed from Lindy's ankle and she was restored to the ranks of the fully mobile, with the recommendation that she should take things easy for a while and have massage to help disperse the bruising which still lingered. She promised faithfully to obey, then promptly forgot all about it in the rush of activity that followed.

Lorenz, having by now been told of her plan to stay and work in Edinburgh, had offered his enthusiastic co-operation. Through him she was introduced to colleagues and supporters of the Edinburgh Festival, and through them the commissions began to flow in. She was asked to do flowers for a twenty-first birthday party, for a wedding, for a formal dinner at a banker's home and, because of that, for a banquet in a fine hall in George Street.

All this was good, but what she needed were regular commissions: flowers to be done once or twice weekly (and preferably daily) in foyers or executive suites. By June these came to her: she got the order for the floral decor in several of the branches of a bank (the more prestigious branches), and from that other orders flowed in, notably from hotels.

So now she had plenty of work. Not quite as much as she could manage, because she wanted to leave a little leeway for the extra orders that would come in over the Festival period.

'I will see you get much work,' Lorenz promised. 'Already, of course, contracts have been signed for the flowers in many places—the Festival Club and the exhibition halls. But I have a friend in the newspaper office who perhaps can put your name forward for the events the newspaper is sponsoring, and then there are many receptions . . .'

'You're *such* a help, darling!'

'It is nothing.' He kissed the top of her head. 'So long as you are encouraged to stay here by these engagements . . .'

She laughed. 'It isn't the "engagements" that keep me here.'

'No? It is me, then?' He was delighted. 'In that case you will stay for ever, not just until after the Festival.'

She made no reply to that. She had no idea as yet how matters were going to go between herself and Lorenz. On her own side, her feelings were a strange mixture; delight in his company, rapture in his kisses, pride in his devotion to her—and yet doubt at the very intensity of her own feelings. She had never felt like this in her life before; never before arranged her career so as to be near a man, never planned her days so as to be able to spend time with him. It was all so new and bewildering—and inescapable.

For Lorenz's part, everything seemed simpler. He adored her: he told her so often. He spent every available moment with her. She knew all about his job—if the Kiev State Choir were laid low by a mysterious virus in Toronto, if the scenery for the Italian State Opera was too big to fit into the transporter, Lindy was the first to hear of it.

It was delightful to be so much part of his life. It made her proud and happy. Yet in a way it frightened her. How could it have happened? Two months ago she had been a London career girl, busy, confident, independent. Now, though she was still busy, she was no longer so confident; so much of her well-being was tied up in another person. Without him she felt incomplete. And as for independence, that had gone! She was ready to rearrange her whole working day, not once but over and over again, just so as to be able to spend an evening with Lorenz or have lunch with him.

It wasn't that she in any way regretted all this; it was simply that it had come about so quickly. It shook to pieces the image she had formed of herself, in the way that the shape in a kaleidoscope is shaken; the new image pleased her—this happy, busy, love-filled girl—but what had happened to the old one of which she used to be so proud?

Her letters to her former flatmate were full of Lorenz. Julia, replying, wrote: 'It's extraordinary. I never thought you were the sort to fall headlong.' Then, obviously thinking that sounded a bit feckless, she had added: 'Maybe you haven't "fallen" so much as got carried away. You don't seem the same girl any more—almost as if you're caught up in some glorious whirlwind!'

The words brought to mind something she had been reading the previous night; unable to sleep after a hectic day, she had borrowed a book from Arnold's shelves, the works of Elizabeth Barrett Browning. As often before, she lingered over the 'Sonnets from the Portuguese'; what Julia now said of her was like the poet's words:

'. . . I, who thought to sink,
Was caught up into love, and taught the whole
Of a new rhythm.'

It was true. Lindy's life had taken on a new rhythm since she met Lorenz—a happier, more breathless rhythm.

But it is difficult to be happy when you see someone else suffering. And Lindy had no doubt that Marion was suffering. Marion's feelings for Lorenz were evidently very deep and fervent; that in itself made it bad enough that she should have been supplanted by another girl. But what made it worse was that, having failed to achieve any success so far as a pianist, Marion had turned to Lorenz as her consolation. And—worse yet—she had no intention of letting go, of bowing out gracefully. She had a good excuse for keeping in contact with him; he was helping to arrange the programme of contemporary music she was going to play during the Festival.

Even if she had wanted to, Lindy couldn't have avoided Marion. Marion was one of those who helped with Arnold's dig at Braco; she was a friend of Rob's; she was, or thought she was, *more* than a friend of Lorenz's. So they were often thrown together.

The first little flare-up occurred one evening at a reception given by the University. An American tycoon had gifted some rare books to the library; the dons had arranged a rather dignified party to welcome him. As a favour, Arnold asked Lindy to provide some flowers, which she did willingly. She herself wouldn't be at the actual reception but was there as the first guests began to gather, to leave two 'Carmen' roses, one each for the wife of the tycoon and their daughter.

To her surprise, she caught sight of Marion's ash-blonde hair among the people grouped at the far end of the room. A movement in the little crowd allowed a gap to show, and she saw a piano; she realized Marion had been asked to play, and that she was now arranging her music on the holder.

She thought no more about it for the moment. Instead she sought out Mrs Kinnair, wife of the University librarian, to ask her to take charge of the roses.

'But how *beautiful*!' Mrs Kinnair burst out when she looked into the box. 'I've never seen anything like it before—roses with different coloured petals!'

Lindy smiled. 'It's not just one blossom,' she explained. 'Each of those boutonnières is made up of the petals of three roses, in different shades of pink.'

'You mean you've put them together petal by petal?'

'Yes. Do you like them?'

'But they're *lovely*, simply *lovely*!' The other woman's plump face quivered with the intensity of her enthusiasm. 'My dear, they must have taken you *ages*!'

'Yes, they are rather time-consuming, but I've done work for Americans before and I know how the women love to be presented with a corsage.'

'They'll *love* these. They're a work of art!' She turned and beckoned to the only other woman who happened to be available—Marion McColl. 'Don't you think these are absolutely out of this world, Marion?'

Marion came close, looked into the box, picked out a buttonhole from its bed of moist tissue. 'Ugh,' she said, 'they're wired. I hate wired flowers—it's so cruel.'

'Oh, my dear, how *absurd*! How else could you achieve the effect, if you didn't—'

'If it were me, I wouldn't bother. A natural flower is much prettier than all this artificiality.' She glanced venomously at Lindy as she spoke.

'As it happens, I agree with you,' Lindy said. 'For myself, I'd rather just keep flowers as simple as possible. But experience as a florist has taught me that the public do like these special effects, especially as a presentation.'

'And speaking for *myself*,' insisted Mrs Kinnair, casting a glare of disapproval at Marion, 'I think those flowers are superb, but *superb*, and I'm sure Mrs Hezzenfell and her daughter will feel the same.'

Lindy smiled her thanks and left. She had a date with Lorenz: he was calling to pick her up from the University. She went out to the door, where she stood for a while watching the June sunlight gleaming on the square, a graceful Georgian precinct with a railed garden in the centre. After a moment she had a sense of being watched. She looked up. At the tall window of the first floor room where the reception was to be held, she glimpsed a face, quickly gone—yet she sensed the watcher was still there. Within a few seconds Lorenz walked up, kissed her in greeting, slipped her arm through his and hurried her away. In her heart Lindy knew that the eyes at the first floor window had witnessed the entire scene.

But she thought no more about it till she got home late that night. Arnold came out to the hall. 'Will you ring Mrs Kinnair, please, Lindy? She's been trying to reach you for more than an hour. Her number is on the telephone pad.'

'Is anything wrong? Did something happen to the flower arrangements?' She was prepared to hear that something had been knocked over and broken.

'Not that I'm aware of.'

Shrugging, she picked up the phone. Mrs Kinnair, who must have been waiting for her, answered at once. 'My *dear*, an absolute tragedy! I blame myself for just being *careless*! Your lovely roses!'

'What about them, Mrs Kinnair?'

'I left them on a table, near the *wine*, because of course I thought we'd take our guests to the buffet almost at once and offer them a drink, and I thought that *then*, first of *all*, I'd present the roses. But my *dear*, they got knocked off the table and *trodden* on!'

'Oh, Mrs Kinnair!'

'I *know*, you're thinking I'm *dreadful*, and I have *no* excuse!' The lamenting voice went on, dipping and falling in over-emphasis at almost every second word.

'Were the flowers in their box?' she interrupted.

'Yes, my dear, because I thought they'd be safer there until the last moment.'

'Then how could they be trodden on?'

'Oh, Lindy dear, one of the *men*, of course, with their great clod-hopping feet! You know how they clump about. Still, it's no use blaming *them*—it's *my* fault, and I do apologize for the waste of all your work.'

'Please don't be unhappy about it, Mrs Kinnair. I'm sure you aren't to blame.' Which was the truth. She was almost certain that the flowers had been destroyed on purpose, and she was equally certain she knew the culprit.

Her first reaction, after she put the phone down, was one of anger. But upstairs in her room she cooled down. She realized that Marion had probably succumbed to a momentary temptation, a spasm of resentment. And then, once it was done, it couldn't be undone. Flowers are so fragile—'like human happiness,' she mused, and then laughed at her herself for her trite philosophising.

She would just forget the incident. The presentation flowers for Mrs Hezzenfell and her daughter had been an idea of her own, and their non-presentation caused no trouble, so nothing was lost (except her afternoon's work). She wouldn't mention it to anyone, not even to Marion.

But it wasn't quite so easy to put it out of her mind. Next day she had an appointment to go to Rob's nursery, to see which of his flowers she might like to use for decor. She drove out to the little village of Cramond in the mini-

van she was hiring at present, following directions
drummed into her by her brother: west along the Queens-
ferry Road, turn off round the Royal Burgess Golf Course,
and then down to the bank of the River Almond. Rob's
place was on the side of the village furthest away from
Edinburgh, between its westernmost houses and the river,
close to a spot known as Peggy's Mill.

She found it without difficulty. As she turned in at the
gates of the nursery she slowed almost to a standstill,
struck by the wave of fragrance from the flowers, a
mingled bouquet from which she could pick out freesia,
border carnation, daphne, Spanish iris, auratum lilies and
Regales. She sat gazing through the windscreen at the
orderly rows of flowers, sheltered from storm and wind by
high hedges of cupressus, tended now by two figures moving carefully among them, a boy and an old man. Behind
the flower-beds were the greenhouses, all alike in design
but some shaded with green semi-opaque blinds. Behind
those again, the house: it looked as if it might once have
been a little farmhouse, built of grey Scottish granite with
a sturdy slate roof, but now trimmed with sparkling white
paintwork at window and door and gable.

She stared at it, and thought, ' How extraordinary.
These last two years, while I've been rushing to and fro
in noisy old London, Rob has been living here in this
... this *sanctuary*.' For that was what it seemed—a place
of peace and tranquillity, cradled in its own flower
perfumes.

She let the Mini roll slowly up the drive. The two
figures working among the flowers straightened to watch
her go by. As she drew up on the gravel between the
front of the house and the greenhouses, a door opened
and Rob came out, drying his hands on a large square of
kitchen towelpaper.

' Hello,' he said. ' I saw you arriving. What do you
think of the old homestead?'

She looked about her. ' Well, it's very calm and neat
... But what struck me was the scent of the flowers ...'

' Ah yes. That's my trademark, you know. All the

florists in Scotland know by now—'' If you want a scented blossom, probably Robert Blair grows it.'' You saw my carnations?'

'Yes, a lovely show—'

'And plenty more in the greenhouses for the autumn and winter markets. Come along—do you want to look now or shall we have coffee first?'

'Oh, please let's look at the flowers!'

'This way. This is the first of the carnation houses—I grow on a two-year programme, of course, and these will be ready for cutting in September.' He waved her in; warmth seemed to pour down from the glass roof although the sky was full of scattered white cloud. The plants were growing in beds edged with concrete, spotlessly clean, not a weed in sight; supports of wire went the length of the beds, to which the stems were tied by a lattice work of string. Each of the plants showed a healthy trio of buds.

'These are Ashington White—there's a big market for those for bridal bouquets. This is Crowley Sim—that's that rosy pink one, you're sure to have used it.' He walked along the path, still damp from the hosing he had just given it. 'This is Ashington again. This is Bailey's Masterpiece. Golden Gleam. King of Cloves. Fragrant Ann.'

She followed as he led the way out of the house, across a path, in at another door. More carnations, at an earlier stage. 'These will be for the Christmas market. A lot of red varieties, naturally. We won't go into the other carnation houses, all you'll see is little green shoots. Come and see the exotics.'

They walked rapidly past a series of greenhouses until they came to one in which the green shades were partly drawn. As he carefully opened the door, an absolutely intoxicating scent poured out.

Lindy gasped, 'Good heavens, it's like being in a perfumed bath, Rob!'

'You get awfully used to it, oddly enough. Come and look at what's causing it all.'

She walked forward to the first bench. On it, in deep troughs, a tall, spiky-stemmed plant was growing, from the tip of which, downward, trumpet-shaped blossoms in increasing size grew in profusion. From the creamy white blooms the fragrance was languorous and rich.

'Tuberoses. I've been very lucky with mine—usually get a dozen blossoms off each plant. Those ten plants will yield a hundred and twenty single tuberoses.'

Lindy gave a muted whistle. As a florist, she knew the wholesale price of one tuberose. Rob gave her a side-long glance, then said blandly, 'Well, they're worth it—they're hard work. Now if you look behind the tuberoses to the trellises, you'll see stephanotis—that's another bridal bouquet favourite, as I don't need to tell you. This way.'

He ushered her on, through one house after another until she was dazed by the parade of beautiful, exotic flowers: gerbena, anthurium, Eucharis lily, bouvardia, gardenia . . .

'Now we're coming to my especial pets,' he said. Once more he opened a door with caution. 'Mustn't ever fling open the door and rush in here—draughts are bad for orchids.'

She was on his heels, but stopped short. 'Oh, *Rob*! Oh, how absolutely gorgeous. Good heavens above, it's magnificent!'

The house was extremely warm; the temperature seemed to her to be up in the eighties and because of the moisture, the atmosphere was heavy. But the luxuriant banks of blossoms, the bursts of colour and strange, winged, waxy petals, the perfume—all were breathtaking.

'Do you like them? I specialise in them—in fact I'm breeding a couple of new ones at the moment which I think may do very well.'

'Oh, Rob, they're marvellous! Look at this dear little cream one!'

'That's cymbidium ebureum—the colour is actually described as "ivory". Smell it.' He took it gently between thumb and forefinger to pull it near. The scent was like raisins.

' Oh, that's nice. What's this one?'

' That's cymbidium insigne Rolfe. All of these are cybidiums and most of them come from Burma—which accounts for the temperature in here.'

' *That's* a gorgeous one, that dark red with the creamy slipper.'

' Yes, that's my new baby. It's a cross between cymbidium Swallow and . . . oh, well, never mind, you don't want to hear all about propagation. You really like it?'

' Oh *yes*. Has anybody used it yet?'

' Used it?'

' For a flower arrangement.'

He shook his head. ' Never been outside this greenhouse.'

' Then may I—? Rob? If I get a special commission, may I have it?'

Smiling, he shrugged. ' Depends when you want it. The blooms don't last for ever.'

' But there will be others when these die?'

' Yes, up till about September.'

' Oh, I hope someone asks me to do something tremendous so I can use them! During the Festival, perhaps. I can just see them, with bleached palm leaves perhaps . . . on a black marble pillar . . . I must watch out for a short pillar of black marble!'

Her enthusiasm made her feel even hotter: perspiration was making her silk shirt stick to her back. ' Can we go outside for a minute?' she asked, and headed for the door.

' Careful!' He put his hand on it to prevent her pulling it open. ' Gently does it. One strong whiff of cold air, and all those crisp petals would go blotchy.' He eased the door open and they went out. ' Come on, it's nearly eleven—let's have that coffee.'

She was thankful to comply, for she found she was very thirsty. Inside the house she offered to make the coffee, but was waved aside by Rob, who produced it in a few minutes from a Cona jug. 'There's always coffee available in this house. I drink it by the gallon. Have a biscuit?'

She shook her head. Her attention was busy, taking in the details of the room. It was the entire ground floor of the old farmhouse except for the kitchen, which still retained its former walls. It was carpeted in charcoal grey, had walls of biscuit-coloured paint, a row of very businesslike filing cabinets along one wall, a desk, two or three chairs, and very little else.

'Are you thinking it's a bit arid?' he inquired. 'Most women say it is.'

'Well, it could do with a few softer touches. Don't you ever bring any of your flowers in?'

'Never. Funnily enough, I always think they look a mess when I put them in a vase. So I look at them on the plants in the greenhouse.' He drank some coffee, then said, 'I hear you had a bit of a disaster over your flowers last night.'

'Who told you that?' she said sharply, surprised.

He paused in the act of putting down his coffee-mug. 'Why? Does it matter?' The tone of her question had clearly puzzled him.

'N-no . . . I just wondered.' She was sure it was Marion who had told him, for who else knew? Yet why should Marion talk to Rob about it? Following her own train of thought, she went on: 'Have you known Marion long?'

'Hmm. Yes, about a year, I suppose. She was doing music at the University, and put her name on the list to help with Arnold's dig—he put up a call for volunteers on the notice board, you see. Quite a lot of students rallied round. She was one of them.'

'So really you've known her longer than Lorenz has.'

'Quite right.' He rubbed the bridge of his nose with his forefinger, a thoughtful, absent-minded gesture, as if while he replied to her his brain was busy on something else.

They finished their coffee. He got up to fetch the

Cona jug from the kitchen. As he refilled the cups h
remarked: 'You know, Marion's been through a ba
time recently.'

'Yes, I'm afraid so.'

'It would be hard to blame her for reacting a bi
violently.'

'I agree.'

'Then you don't blame her?'

'For what?'

'For doing whatever it was she did last night.'

'Didn't she tell you what she did?'

'Marion? Why on earth should she?'

'But I thought—' She broke off, colouring. 'Didn'
you say Marion told you there was an accident to th
flowers?'

'No, *you* said that, or at least implied it.'

'You mean she didn't tell you?'

'I haven't exchanged a word with Marion since tha
meeting at your brother's house about extending th
excavation.'

'But . . . but . . . how did you know about th
accident, then?'

'I *don't* know. I'm still waiting for you to tell me
Arnold rang me this morning about transport for th
weekend's trip to Braco. He just said Mrs Kinnair ha
been in a tizz last night and that something seemed t
have gone wrong. When I mentioned it to you, I wa
simply making conversation.'

'Oh.' If anything, her colour was even deeper now

'What did happen?'

'It doesn't matter. I'd decided to forget about it.

'But you think Marion was responsible.'

'Yes, I do.'

'You could be wrong, though?'

'I suppose so, but I don't think so.'

Rob brought his light blue eyes to rest on her with a
steady, level scrutiny. 'I think, in the circumstances
Marion is entitled to the benefit of the doubt. What's
been happening the last few weeks is likely to make he

66

. . . antagonistic, to say the least.' His voice sank a tone or two. ' I speak from experience.'

Lindy wanted to rejoin: ' But you didn't do anything spiteful.' But the conversation was difficult enough without going into *that*. She said in a rather muffled voice, ' I assure you I don't want to hurt Marion in any way.'

'Good. Drink up your coffee and we'll go and look at the rest of the orchids. I've got some dendrobium that I think you'll like, nearly finished flowering for this year, but you might like to bear them in mind for next spring for bridal bouquets—dendrobium formosum, a very pure white . . .' He talked on with determination about orchids, and by the time she had seen the other orchid-house and been carried away, as before, by their beauty, she had almost forgotten the episode.

It came back to her mind, though, during the following weekend. She herself couldn't go to the dig at Braco on the Friday evening or the Saturday because she had commitments in Edinburgh—Saturday was always her busiest day. Besides, she had a date with Lorenz for Friday evening and Saturday lunch. But on Sunday Lorenz had to play host to the concert manager of the Kiev Choir and his interpreter, so Lindy took herself off to Perthshire.

She was astounded at the scenery that met her eyes as she drove north. She crossed the Forth by the slender, soaring new bridge, then took a turn west through a range of hills, green and rolling, dotted with sheep and occasional farms but on the whole empty—even the road wasn't particularly busy compared with the traffic to be found on a fine June Sunday in the South of England.

She followed the signposts for Dunblane, joined a motorway north of Stirling, left it again according to instructions when she saw the river called the Alan Water, and presently found herself gentling the Mini along the main street of Braco, looking for the turning on the right where, so she'd been told, she would find a place off the main traffic route to park her car.

She was hailed by a voice from somewhere above her. She leaned out and looked up, to find Arnold on a bank of turf above the road, looking hot and dishevelled in khaki drill trousers and a bush shirt.

'A few yards up on the right,' he called. 'You'll see the other cars. You can come on the site by the track through the thicket, but mind how you go.'

She waved acknowledgement. A few minutes later she was scrambling up the incline where she had seen her brother, who was now bent over a photostat plan of the section on which they were working. Two young men, muddy and rumpled, were listening and nodding as he talked.

'All right, it may only be a paving-stone,' he was saying, 'but on the other hand it may be a stone postern-gate, in which case it may have engravings of the legion's standards. So until you get it out, no spades, no trowels, no hard tools—hands and wooden spatulas only. Right?'

'Right.'

Lindy joined him as they walked purposefully away. 'Found something?'

'I don't really think so. It's a big slab of dressed stone, probably part of the paving of the outer defence post. Well, what do you think of it?'

Lindy followed the sweep of his hand, and was impressed. They were standing on a turf-covered slope which quite clearly was a wall buried under soil and grass; it stretched for yards to either side of them. It was easy to trace a series of squares and bays, which had been the defence walls of the fortress, one inside the other. Between the sequence of walls there were moats or ditches which presumably had held water. In the centre the outlines of buildings could still be seen.

The excavation was going on on a section of the outer wall. A blue tent was set up there, together with some trestle tables and canvas chairs. It was easy to pick out Marion's figure, in dark blue poplin pants and shirt; she was sitting at the table, talking to someone with his back to Lindy.

'Wander round and take a look,' Arnold invited.

'What would you like me to do?'

'Whatever you fancy. Marion's keeping the catalogue, and Sheila's doing the labelling—not that we've got anything much to label so far. The two other girls are on the dig, but it's hard work—your knees give out after a while. Go and see what you think.'

She made her way along the dyke, glad that she had chosen to wear thick-soled crêpe loungers, and slacks to protect her legs from the gorse and thistle that grew everywhere. As she reached the table where Marion was sitting, she realised that the man talking to her was Rob.

He had a basket of earth in his arms. Their heads were bent over it. With a rather grimy forefinger Rob was easing out pieces of red tile.

'Roof tiles . . .' he was saying as Lindy came up. 'At least that's what Arnold says. But he can't understand why there should be tiles here because most of the fortress is thought to have had thatch.'

'Does he want me to catalogue them?'

'Every piece. Sheila's got the bits we've already sorted out and she's docketing them. I'll bring them over when she's finished.' He straightened, easing his back muscles. As he did so he saw Lindy. 'Well, hello! You've just arrived in nice time. We've got a long and fiddly job on—we've found some red tile in about six million pieces.'

'Yes, I heard. What do you want me to do?'

'How do you fancy sitting here with Sheila and Marion to help with the cataloguing?'

'Yes, fine. But first can I see the actual dig?'

'Come on then, you'd better speak to Hamish. He's Arnold's right-hand man.'

Hamish took her under his wing to show her what was being done in the trench: the careful uncovering of layers of earth leading at last to the platform on which the sentries had stood, the laying aside of every stone,

69

shard, or fragment, the painstaking work with camel-hair brushes, with drops of water, with magnifying glasses to see if any surfaces would yield clues.

'It's really a drudgery,' he said cheerfully. 'Half the time all you get is rotten old earth and stones. But there's always the hope that you might find something good—a sword, maybe, or a drinking vessel.'

'Have you ever been on a dig where you found anything good?'

'Not myself, personally—but I helped on the dig at Sief Le Brun, in Alsace, when they found that mosaic.'

Lindy had never heard of Sief Le Brun or its mosaic, but nodded appreciatively and was shown what the Braco dig had to offer—a fairly deep trench about twelve feet long with three men working in it, two girls gently lifting soil into baskets, three other men, including Rob, acting as jack-of-all-trades, and Arnold fussing over them all. Sheila had by now joined Marion at the trestle table. Lindy, after strolling about for ten minutes, was finally made to feel guilty at her idleness, so went to begin work on the catalogue.

The time sped past. At one o'clock the girls broke off and began preparations for lunch. Lindy gained a great deal of popularity by taking two of the men to her Mini and showing them the large box of ice she had brought, containing tins of shandy and lager and a very big double-wrapped polythene bag containing salmon mayonnaise and salad. Sheila had already been to the village at crack of dawn for milk and rolls. Considering that it was almost entirely impromptu, it was a very successful meal.

When they resumed at two-thirty, the sun was very hot. There was no immediate shade—the nearest trees were some fifty yards away. The girls made themselves paper hats from pages of the Sunday papers, but even so it was warm work. Dust from the fragments of tile rose in a little cloud over the trestle table; Lindy could feel it clinging to the loose tendrils of her hair and caking her forehead. The other girls, when she looked at them, had streaks of dust in the perspiration on their foreheads. But it didn't occur to any of them to stop.

About five o'clock there was a spontaneous decision to break for tea. Sheila put the kettle on to boil over the camping-gas heater. As they were setting out cups and mugs, Lindy saw Marion stare past her shoulder, eyes wide.

She knew almost without having to turn around that Lorenz had arrived.

'Hello, how hot and tired you all look! Lindy, *mein Schatz*, you have dust all over your nose.'

'Have I?' She put up a hand to brush it away.

'That only makes it worse. Ah, you should not be doing such a thing on a hot day!'

'I didn't realise you'd be free today, Lorenz?'

'Neither did I. But Mr Akimirov, after lunch, decided he would like to be shown round Edinburgh Castle. And as I do not know anything about Edinburgh Castle, I gave him to James Reidpath, of the Scottish Orchestra, who agrees to tell him of the history. And so I thought I would come to take you out to dinner.'

'Like this?' Lindy laughed.

'No, naturally, not like that, although I like the dark blouse with the little white flowers . . .' He became aware that the girl beyond Lindy, shaded under the absurd paper hat, was Marion. 'Ah, good afternoon, Marion. And Sheila too, is it not?'

'Hello, Lorenz.'

'That's good timing,' Arnold observed as he joined them. 'We're just about to have tea, Lorenz.'

'Tea—the British always stop for tea,' he laughed. 'It is just as well. You all look fatigued.'

'Well, it isn't a rest cure, working on a dig.'

'I can see that it is not.' He turned to survey Marion with concern. 'It is not good for the hands of a pianist, surely, Marion.'

If he had given her a million pounds she couldn't have looked more radiant. 'It's nice of you to bother, Lorenz.'

'But I mean what I say. Digging is certainly not good.'

'Oh, I don't do any digging. Only the clerical work.'

'Ah. That is not so bad.' Having satisfied himself on that score, he turned his attention back to Lindy. 'After tea we will go back to Edinburgh, yes? I have telephoned for a table at the Tolbooth Hotel, for eight o'clock. That gives you time to get home and change.'

'Oh, no, Lorenz, I promised to help on the dig today.'

'But you have done enough, surely? You have been here since the morning?'

'Yes.'

'And now it is after five. And you look so tired.'

'Well, I am, I suppose, but not more than anyone else.'

'I don't like to see you look tired, *Liebling*. Come, she has done enough, has she not, Arnold?'

'One isn't a slave-driver,' said Arnold. 'She's free to go if she wants to.'

'Nothing would ever get done here if we all got up and walked away,' Marion remarked in a cool voice.

'I quite agree,' Lindy said. 'I really intended to—'

'But you could easily be persuaded to change your mind.'

'Why should she not change her mind?' Lorenz demanded. 'If it is all done of the free will. And she *does* look tired.'

'We're all tired, Lorenz.' Marion's voice was very sharp now.

Rob intervened. 'I think few of us get up as early as Lindy,' he pointed out. 'She has to be at the flower market by six most mornings. Am I right, Lindy?'

She nodded. Lorenz smiled, put his arm protectively around her, and somehow it was settled that after tea she would be leaving for town. She still felt a bit guilty about it when she saw the others washing up their cups and mugs and preparing to get down to it again. Marion, she noted, was already very busy at her end of the trestle, head bent low over a trayful of fragments.

72

As she collected up her handbag, Arnold said, ' Thanks for your help. Have a nice evening.'

' You don't mind my going now?'

' Of course not.' He glanced at Marion. ' It would have been better if Lorenz hadn't turned up, though.'

' I'm sorry, Arnold, I didn't know he was coming.'

' Never mind, one can't foresee everything.' He watched as Rob came up and took the canvas chair next to Marion. ' Luckily,' he added, ' she isn't without friends.'

That remark troubled her all through the evening, so much so that Lorenz said to her, ' You are very quiet, Lindy.'

' Maybe it's just that I'm tired, as you said.'

' And maybe it is also that your brother and his friends make too many claims on you. It seems to me, darling, that we hardly ever have time to talk seriously together.'

' Have we anything " serious " to say to each other?' she asked, her heart beating faster.

' *Natürlich*. But this is not the time or the place.' He made a little gesture at the busy restaurant, one of the ' in ' places at present since the opening of the hotel, recently converted from a steep old house just off the Royal Mile.

She waited. She wanted him to go on, to say that he had plans for their future together which must be discussed. But all he said at length was, ' We shall think about it. In a few weeks there might be an opportunity . . . I have a business appointment which would fit rather well . . .'

Into what? He didn't finish the sentence, but she found herself hoping he was trying to look forward to a date when they might get married. As the Festival drew nearer, he would grow more and more hectically busy; it was June now, so there was no use imagining a wedding before, say, October, when the Festival was over.

She might tell herself there was no use imagining— but her fancy took flight. An old church—the fine old square-towered church near Arnold's cottage, perhaps; its calm, plain interior lightened by big white urns full of white and yellow flowers—daphne mezereum, perhaps, if she could get some, and yellow roses . . .

Nothing happened to mar this dream as she was taken home; Lorenz's kiss as he said goodnight was full of a passion that made it seem all the brighter.

She went indoors; it wasn't very late, only a little after ten. Arnold was in the sitting-room poring over his log-book of the dig, still in the drill trousers and bush shirt.

'Hmph,' he grunted as she came in. 'Was that Romeo who just drove away?'

She drew back. The gentle dream she had been treasuring shrivelled and vanished at his words.

'If you mean Lorenz, yes, it was.'

He looked up. She could see he was genuinely surprised at her curt reaction. 'What's the matter?'

'Need you call him Romeo?'

'Did I? Oh, sorry—my mind was elsewhere.'

'Is that how you think of him unconsciously?'

'I never think of him at all, my dear girl.'

'You don't? You have your mind on other, more important things.'

Arnold peered at her. Then he took off his glasses and began to polish them on one of the special little blue tissues he used. 'Since you bring it up—yes, one has more important things to consider than Lorenz Hemer.'

'You don't like him?'

'That is a question based on a false premise. One would have to—'

'Oh, for goodness' sake!' she flared. 'Do stop talking about yourself as if you were some sort of disembodied power from out of space. If you mean "I", say "I"!'

'My manner of speech irritates you? Perhaps I—'

'And that isn't all that does! What gives you the right to judge Lorenz and find him wanting? You scarcely know him.'

'I could say the same of you,' he replied. 'In fact I have known him longer than you.'

'But never got to know him well.'

'No, but then I'm not in a haze of romantic emotion, as you are, my dear. I see Lorenz clearly—'

'I very much doubt that—'

'—As *you* will,' he went on inexorably, 'when you get over this extraordinary involvement. You'll grow out of it, Lindy—'

'How dare you!' She was extremely angry now, at his assumption that she was being juvenile. 'I'm quite old-enough to choose my own friends, thank you, without any opinions from you!'

'We're not talking of mere friendship, Lindy.'

'No, and that's what's at the back of it all. You still can't forgive me because I turned my back on the man you'd chosen, and say what you like you still have hopes—'

'If you're talking about Rob, let me advise you—'

'I don't need your advice! At least in Lorenz I've found a man who makes his own decisions and leads his own life—unlike Rob, who does seem to need your advice from the way he keeps his life running alongside yours. You have him in your pocket! Has he no mind of his own?'

'Lindy, I really must warn you—'

'What makes you think I need warnings and advice? You can't be so conceited as to think—'

There was a flurry of sound from the little hall, the banging of the front door, and quick footsteps receding on the cobbled lane. Lindy, stopped short in her tirade, gazed at her brother.

'Who was that?' she gasped.

Arnold sighed and got up from his chair to look out of the window. Shaking his head, he turned back.

'If you had only let me finish what I was trying to say—! The advice and the warning I was trying to give you was that Rob was across the hall in the kitchen, making coffee for us.'

She was aghast. 'And . . . and he heard?'

'When you take into consideration that all the doors were open, and the fact that he left without saying good-night, I think, sister dear, you can be sure he heard.'

There was nothing left to say. All the anger and indignation had gone out of her. Appalled at the words she'd used about Rob, she ran up to her room feeling she might burst into tears.

Not that tears would make it any better.

CHAPTER V

If Lindy hadn't by now become so firmly established in her career in Edinburgh, she would have packed up and moved out. She felt she would never know how to face Rob again if he came to the house.

But all her equipment was in the loft over the garage. The address at which she could be contacted was here at the cottage, her telephone was the number of Arnold's telephone, and the invaluable Mrs Ramsay was usually around if she was out, to take messages. To move elsewhere immediately was well-nigh impossible; she had a diary full of commissions so that she was too busy to look for new premises and negotiate for them.

When she came back from market next morning to find Arnold at breakfast, she stumblingly attempted to put the problem before him.

'Don't be silly. I shouldn't think Rob will come here for quite a long time, in the circumstances.'

'Arnold, I'm sorry.'

'It's not me you should be saying that to, it's Rob.'

'I know that, but I apologise for what I said to you, Arnold. I was very rude to you and very unkind about your friend.'

To her surprise he laughed. 'You sound just like a ten-year-old schoolgirl. "Dinna fash yoursel'", as they're fond of saying hereabouts—meaning don't get in a state. Never forget, Lindy, that I'm trained in the disciplines of archaeology—I see things in a different perspective from you. I know from looking at history that time passes and people change. A little bit of a row doesn't bother me nearly as much as it seems to bother you.'

'I hope Rob sees it like that,' she said remorsefully.

She knew she should go to see him: apologise, explain that she had been carried away by rancour. But she couldn't. Two or three times she picked up the phone and dialled his number, but always put it down again before he answered. She tried to write him a note, but it looked so unconvincing when set down in black and white; she decided to try again tomorrow, but was too busy, and so the days went by, and the whole thing began to fade from her mind.

When at last they met again, two weeks had gone past. There was a briefing by one of the Public Relations Officers of Edinburgh Corporation, to explain about the special flowers and shrubs in Princes Street Gardens during the Festival and other related topics. Since it might influence any decorative effects she herself wanted to try—and in any case she was interested—Lindy went along. Almost at once she saw Rob.

If she had known he was to be there, she might not have gone. As things turned out, it was all for the best. He nodded a greeting, went on with what he was saying to his neighbour, and that was that. As they came out of the City Chambers they were almost shoulder to shoulder.

A fine, bright summer rain was falling. When Lindy set out the day had been fine, so she was wearing a dark muslin dress with lace at the collar and cuffs, quite unsuitable for wet weather. She hesitated in the doorway.

'Can I give you a lift?' Rob offered.

'Oh—no, thanks, my car is parked just the other side of the Bridges—I was just wondering how to get there without being soaked.'

'Why not have a cup of tea till it clears up? It's only a shower.'

'Yes, that would be lovely. Thank you, Rob.'

He looked faintly embarrassed. 'I didn't mean "us", I meant "you"—I can't stop.'

It was her turn to redden. 'Rob, I'd like to say—'

'Some other time, Lindy. I'm really awfully sorry, but I must dash—I'm meeting Marion.' With a little movement of his hand like a salute, he dashed off into the rain, to where his car was parked somewhere the other side of the Mercat Cross.

She sighed and then smiled. The ordeal was over. They had met, she had told him by her manner that she wanted to apologise, and he had waved it aside. Quite clearly he had forgiven her. '*Again*,' her conscience said. So be it—he had forgiven her *again*. She would make certain never to say or do anything that might hurt him in the future.

He had said he was meeting Marion. That struck her as strange. Why should Rob be meeting Marion? When they had had the conversation about Marion spoiling the flowers, he had seemed astonished that she should think Marion ever spoke to him except casually. Yet now he was 'meeting Marion'.

She shrugged. It was really none of her business.

That conclusion proved difficult to maintain, though, as the month of July went by. After that first encounter at the Corporation briefing, fate seemed to throw her into Rob's company continually. Perhaps it was because they were both in the flower business and, as visitors and overseas tourists poured into the city, there was more work for both of them within the same ambience. Almost everywhere Lindy went, she saw Rob; and when she saw Rob, she generally saw Marion with him.

She said one evening to her brother, 'Remember you said to me that Marion isn't without friends?'

'Did I?' Arnold countered. 'When was that?'

'The Sunday at the dig—when Lorenz arrived unexpectedly.'

'Ah yes.'

'Did you know at that time that there was something going between her and Rob?'

Arnold put his finger in his book to mark the place on closing it. 'I certainly didn't, because I don't even know it now. Is there " something going "?'

'Of course there is. They're always around together.'

'I'm aware, of course, that Rob sees her from time to time—'

'I'd call it more like " all the time ".'

He carefully put a marker in the book, since it was

clear that the conversation was going to take longer than he had at first supposed. There was an air of patient forbearance about him. 'What exactly is the point of this inquiry, Lindy?'

She hardly knew herself. She said haltingly, 'I just wondered . . . if maybe Rob had felt sorry for her.'

'I should think that is highly likely.'

'And perhaps had got more involved than he intended.'

He gave her a quizzical look. 'I'd say he was well able to take care of himself. Wouldn't you?'

'Ye . . es.'

'No one could blame him for being attracted to Marion. That type of petite beauty brings out the protective instinct. Even in me.'

'So you don't think we should do anything.'

'Such as what?'

'I don't exactly know. Rob pays a lot of attention to what you say. If you were to—'

'Lindy, I wish you would rid yourself of that delusion. Rob does *not* pay a lot of attention to me.'

'But he—'

'We've known each other a long time and we're good friends. But I have no influence over Rob and never did have.'

'But when he and I got engaged . . .'

'What? What about it?'

'*You* wanted it.'

'Of course I did. Because *he* wanted it.' He threw himself impatiently back in his chair. 'How often do I have to spell it out? You seem determined to stick to that misapprehension of yours! Rob was, and is, my friend. He wanted to marry you. Because of that I urged you into it. But it was Rob's idea, not mine. And now it's Rob's idea to fall in love with Marion—it *certainly* isn't mine!'

'I'm sorry, Arnold. Don't be cross. I just was a bit worried about it. Marion is so intense, isn't she?'

'Perhaps Rob enjoys that. In comparison, you

know.'

'Oh,' Lindy said, biting her lip. The implication was obvious; compared with her own lukewarm affections of two years ago, perhaps Rob felt he had found something better.

Well, she told herself, so had she. The feelings that Lorenz had aroused in her were quite different from anything she had ever experienced. She gloried in them, often telling herself she must be the luckiest girl alive. Here she was, head over heels in love with a man who clearly adored her, spending this beautiful summer in one of the most splendid cities in the world, working at a craft which she enjoyed, and heading towards a marriage that would be as perfect as the courtship.

In a way, knowing that Rob had found someone else seemed to set her free finally. And that Rob should have found Marion . . . that made it like a miracle, because now she need no longer feel guilty, need no longer feel that shadow between herself and Lorenz when they kissed.

On a Monday at the end of July Lorenz rang her. 'We meet for dinner. I have something important to say!'

'Oh, yes, Lorenz!' She had a commission for that evening, but she could see to it before six o'clock, leaving herself time to bath and change for this important announcement. She was sure it was about getting married.

She dressed with care. She had a new two-piece, a long skirt of jade-coloured velvet with a bolero to match; with it she wore a stiff silk blouse with a choker collar. No jewellery, except for the old silver comb she put in her hair, which she plaited into a thick pigtail to hang down her back.

When she surveyed herself in her mirror she thought the effect was good. When she walked into the foyer of the restaurant and saw Lorenz's eyes light up, she knew he approved.

He too was looking his best; he liked to wear a dinner

jacket, and tonight he was wearing one of very dark blue wild silk with a pale blue shirt. With his tawny hair and erect carriage, he was quite the handsomest man in the room.

They were shown to a table in one of the candlelit alcoves. They ordered the meal, and then when the waiter was gone he took her hand.

'Now, my love, you know I said to you that we didn't have enough time together in this busy life we lead.'

'I remember, Lorenz.'

'So now, this weekend, I have to go to London. I have to see the Russian *chargé d'affaires*—I have an appointment for Saturday morning.'

'Yes?' Lindy said, puzzled.

'I give you time enough? You can cancel any appointments you have for Friday and Saturday?'

Light dawned. 'You mean you want me to come with you?'

'But of course! That way we shall have two whole days to ourselves, except for perhaps two hours that I spend at the Embassy on Saturday—and you could fill two hours in London, I am sure.' He looked smilingly at her, questioning her.

'Oh yes, of course.' So that was the important thing he had to say! She tried very hard to control her expression, but her disappointment must have shown, because he looked at her with alarm.

'You don't want to come?'

'Yes, yes, I do, Lorenz. Of course I do.'

He sighed in relief. 'That is better. I thought you were going to say it was not what you would like.'

'Oh, darling, how can you be so silly!' She squeezed his hand. 'Two days to ourselves—to spend as we like without having to rush off to other engagements—it'll be heavenly!' She was angry with herself for almost spoiling things. Why should she imagine that Lorenz's train of thoughts must be a duplicate of her own? Just because she was dreaming about an autumn wedding—!

'I don't know London very well,' he was saying, 'I have been there several times, but only when I was a concert pianist. I know the Festival Hall, the Wigmore Hall . . . one or two hotels . . .'

'It'll be fun to show you London. We'll go to Portobello Road, and to the top of the Post Office Tower.'

'We shall fly, yes? I will book the flight—Friday evening, and then we have time for dinner in London. You will know a good restaurant.'

'Oh, of course. Do you like French food? Greek?'

''S macht nichts. Now tell me, your flat is where?'

'My flat? Oh, in London. Well, I don't know whether you can still call it my flat. Julia has let my room to another girl, but I daresay she can put me up just for the weekend.'

'Ah, so there are other girls there. That would not be very convenient. Better, I think, we book in a hotel. There was a very good hotel I stayed in once, I remember. In Bayswater, it was called. Is that right? Bayswater?'

'That's right, darling,' she laughed.

'Good, good, then. I ring them tomorrow morning to reserve a room.'

'Two rooms, you mean, Lorenz.' But as soon as she had said it, she knew that wasn't what he meant.

At this providential moment the waiter arrived with the first course; in the discussion of who was having the chilled melon, and the setting of fish knife and fork for Lorenz's smoked trout, she had a few moments in which to recover from the shock.

How could she have been so naïve? When Lorenz spoke of a weekend in London, naturally he didn't mean a boy-and-girl, hand-in-hand episode.

And she had thought she was coming to dinner with him to hear a proposal of marriage!

Well, what was she to do now? Was she going to say yes or no? In effect, she had already said yes, by talking about showing him London and remarking that Julia would probably be able to put her up. If she backed out now, he would understand why—it would be blatantly obvious.

She felt a wave of panic. What was she to *do*? She had never imagined herself faced with a problem like this. She didn't want to embark on an affair, even though she knew that before long she would be Lorenz's wife. She felt that everything would be spoilt if she fell in with his plans.

But to say categorically: ' No, Lorenz, I won't come away with you now that I understand what you mean'—she sensed that it would lead to a terrible quarrel.

She didn't want to oppose him in any way. She basked in the warmth of his smile, suffered when he was worried, was sensitive to every one of his moods. If she made him angry or resentful she knew her days would be overshadowed by black clouds.

Lorenz, quite oblivious of the shock she had experienced and the whirl of thoughts in her head, was commenting on the food. ' We had better have hock with the chicken, don't you agree? Or would you prefer a white Bordeaux? That might be lighter—the hocks on the wine list seem to be rather full. What do you prefer, darling?'

' The . . . the Bordeaux.'

' Quite right, it will be better.' He beckoned the wine waiter, gave the order, then turned his attention back to Lindy. ' We might go to a concert on Saturday evening. Or the opera, perhaps. I will see what is being performed. Then we shall have a late-night supper somewhere, yes? It will be very romantic—I can picture it all.'

Luckily he seemed not to notice that her replies were very scant. She simply couldn't put more than two words together: to join in his enthusiastic planning was impossible, and to say ' I've changed my mind, I'm not going!' was even worse.

The meal was excellent. Afterwards they went to the home of a musician who was having a late-night-music party: here the need for conversation was removed.

When Lorenz at last took her home, nothing had been said to mar his idea that the coming weekend was something they both looked forward to.

He took her in his arms to say goodnight. As his lips caressed her cheek and her throat, she felt for the first time, with him, that dreadful dismay that she had experienced once before, with Rob. It sprang from the knowledge that here was a man who wanted her to give herself to him completely.

And for the first time she didn't respond to Lorenz's kiss. She tried to: she tried to put out of her mind the foolish sense of shock and disappointment she'd felt earlier. But something was changed in their relationship and she was not quite enough of an actress to hide it.

'Ah, you are tired, *mein Schätzchen*. I forgot that you have to get up so very early and your day is so long.' He let her go with gentleness, then kissed her very softly on the lips. 'Goodnight, then. Dream of me!'

She stood on tiptoe to kiss him in return. Though he didn't know it, it was a kiss of gratitude—that he hadn't guessed the real reason for her passivity, that he hadn't taken her to task.

She went indoors. When he had driven off she stood for a long time in the little hall. She knew she wouldn't sleep if she went to bed. After a few moments she went out again, and up to her workroom over the garage.

Here the containers for tomorrow's work stood ready. The foliage for two of the big designs she would do were in a deep container of water; the sharp smell of the leaves of Portugal laurel, whitebeam and eucalyptus came to her. She moved towards the container, touching the branches with adroit fingers, feeling the health and vigour of the leaves. In the morning—in only four or five hours—she would go to market for the gladioli, columbine and fritillaries that would form the main mass of the shapes she had in mind for the lecture hall where they would stand—grave, dignified, imposing, suitable for a conference of international architects. And the designs for the lunch tables—low and narrow, so that the men could see each other without looking around a flower vase . . .

She became aware that the shapes of the leaves were blurring in front of her eyes. She blinked back the tears.

Fool! Stupid, romantic, self-centred fool! Because she'd been satisfied with her own little dream, did it follow that Lorenz was? She faced the fact that a man's needs are different: she remembered reading somewhere —in the works of the poet Coleridge—a sentence that seemed to sum it all up. ' The man's desire is for the woman; but the woman's desire is rarely other than for the desire of the man.'

She experienced a feeling that was almost despair. Was there something wrong with her? Was she incapable of feeling real love? Twice in her life she had not only failed to respond—she had actually felt herself recoil—when a man expected more than juvenile romancing. Was she inadequate? Immature? Everything seemed to point to that. Other girls of her age seemed to take the vagaries of love in their stride, some of them falling in and out of love with an enthusiasm she found astonishing. Julia, for instance, her former flat-mate: men came and went in Julia's life, and sometimes she was happy and sometimes she was sad, but she never seemed to doubt herself. What she did, she did wholeheartedly.

' Why,' Lindy asked herself in torment, ' why can't I be like that?'

She might excuse it to herself by saying that she was fastidious, reticent, discriminating . . . But those words simply covered up the fact that she was a coward.

She always had been, it seemed. And apparently she always would be unless she took the plunge now. Why not? She loved Lorenz, and he loved her: that should be enough to justify their behaviour.

Unheeded, the hours went by. She became aware that a clock was striking—she raised her head to listen. Three o'clock! And at five she must be up and out to go to the Waverley Market. She *must* get some sleep.

But when she had undressed and washed, she knew it was hopeless to go to bed. She was too keyed up for sleep. She went down from her room, put on the kettle, and made herself a cup of tea. She was pouring it when she heard a heavy tread on the stairs just before her brother put his head round the kitchen door.

'What on earth . . . ? Lindy, do you realize it's nearly half past three?'

She nodded.

'What's the matter? Aren't you feeling well?'

'No, I'm all right. I just don't seem to be sleepy.'

'Good heavens above, child, neither you will be if you drink tea in the middle of the night. Hot milk would be far better.'

'I suppose so. I just felt like a cup of tea, that's all. Would you like one?'

'I suppose so, since I'm here.'

'I'm sorry I woke you, Arnold.'

He shrugged. Without his glasses, and with his hair rumpled, he looked quite different—less composed and masterful. He took his cup from her, put in four sugar lumps, and stirred thoughtfully, eyeing her while he did so. 'Are you sure you're all right? You're very pale.'

'I'm fine, thanks.'

'Then why can't you sleep?'

'I've . . . I've got things on my mind.'

'Quarrelled with your boy-friend?'

'No,' she returned at once, 'of course not. What makes you say that?'

'I don't know. If a girl can't sleep, it seems a natural conclusion that she might be having what I believe is called " man trouble ". Are you?'

She gave a wry smile. 'I certainly have a slight problem. But it's on my side—so I suppose you'd call it " woman trouble ".'

'And you've quarrelled with Lorenz about it?'

'No, I haven't. He doesn't even know the problem exists.'

Her brother blinked. 'Maybe it's because it's the middle of the night, but I don't believe I follow that. But then it's probably to do with emotion. One isn't perhaps qualified—I mean, *I* am perhaps not qualified to judge emotions.'

She studied him with, for the first time, a curiosity about his personal life. 'Have you ever thought about getting married, Arnold?'

'I've thought about it.'

'You mean there have been women you'd have liked to marry?'

'Oh, not in large numbers. One, perhaps.'

'And why didn't you?'

Arnold pushed the sugar bowl about with one finger, watching it intently as he did so. Lindy realised with amazement that he was embarrassed. It never occurred to her that her brother could be embarrassed. 'I'm sorry,' she said quickly. 'It's no business of mine.'

'No, but it's natural you should be interested. The trouble with me, Lindy, is that to women I seem such a dry old stick.'

'Oh, Arnold!'

'Well, don't I? All bound up in my archaeological work, heading past my mid-thirties, getting more professorial every week . . . When a girl compares me with other men—with your Lorenz, for instance, or Rob —don't I seem a bit of a bore?'

'Arnold *dear*, how can you say—'

'You know yourself you think I'm bossy and lacking in warmth. Tell the truth, Lindy—until this moment it never occurred to you that I could want a wife and a family just like other men.'

She sighed. 'But that's only because I seem to be so selfishly taken up with my own affairs. Any other sister would have been trying to marry you off ages ago.'

'And who would you marry me off to?' he parried, his brown eyes beginning to twinkle.

'Oh . . . well . . . let me think.' Wildly she cast about for a suitable wife for Arnold, but the only mental images

88

she came up with were faculty wives like Mrs Kinnair—
settled, steady, unglamorous.

' You see, you can't think of anyone. I think women
don't regard me as the marrying kind.'

' But you are?'

' I think I am.'

' And what kind of girl would you like to marry?'

' That's easy. Someone who would give me her whole
heart if she decided to love me—someone who has all the
qualities I lack—deep feelings, sensitivity, ardour . . .
And pretty too, and intelligent . . .' He chuckled. ' It's
not asking much, is it!'

She looked at him with a troubled gaze. His immediate response to her question seemed to imply that there
actually was a woman whom he loved. Who could it
be? Certainly no one Lindy had ever met, or at least
if she had met her there had been no sign of any feelings between them. Poor Arnold! Could he possibly be
hopelessly in love?

A silence fell between them, a thoughtful silence.
Presently Lindy said: ' If you were in love and the girl
loved you, you'd want to get married.'

' Of course.' He frowned.

' I mean, you wouldn't want to have an affair?'

At that he laughed outright. ' My dear *girl*, can you
imagine me in all the jiggery-pokery of an affair? I hate
that sort of thing. Life's complicated enough without
getting involved with lies and pretences and so on. If a
man loves a woman and she loves him and there are no
obstacles in the way, it seems to me that the accepted,
sensible thing is to get married. Anything else is a sort
of sham. Maybe I'm conventional . . . but then I think
conventions grew up because they made a good frame-
work for ordinary, honest living. Don't you?'

' I suppose so.' What else had she expected from
Arnold? He was not the sort to recommend throwing
your bonnet over the windmill. He had only reinforced
her own view. Her shoulders sagged.

' Come on, off to bed. You really must get some

rest.'

Obediently she got up. When she laid her head on her pillow she fell asleep almost at once from sheer exhaustion but only minutes later, it seemed, her alarm clock was shrilling. She muffled it under her pillow for fear of disturbing Arnold again, and clambered out of bed, so weary still that her body seemed to ache.

The wholesalers in Cockburn Street and Market Street were already bustling about when she arrived, muffled in a quilted nylon jacket and headscarf against the sharp dawn breeze. Behind her the Castle loomed, black against an oyster-coloured sky. Gulls rose, crying, from the grassy slopes of the Mound where they had perched to watch the sunrise. The world had that strange feel about it—hesitant, expectant.

She walked up the slope towards East Market Street. There, parked by the premises of a flower merchant, was the little cream van that Rob Blair used for deliveries. Rob himself was not to be seen. She went into the showroom of her usual supplier to collect the fritillaries and gladioli she had ordered. Columbines there were none: 'They dinna grow them much up here, Miss Gramont, and in the south they're finished, ye see,' she was told apologetically. 'I tried to get some sent up on the railway, but it was no use.'

'Never mind, Mr Miller, it doesn't matter. Have you got some dark red larkspur, and some sweet peas?'

'Aye, larkspur, but no sweet peas. You'll mebbe get them from Davidson, or—hi, Mr Blair! Mr Blair!' The dealer darted out of the shop to buttonhole Rob as he passed by. 'Mr Blair, this young lady's wanting sweet peas—'

'Sorry, I've sold all—Oh, hello, Lindy, it's you!'

'Hello, Rob. You're the very man. Have you got anything with a soft-petalled bloom on a slender stem, like aquilegia? I was hoping to get some, but Mr Miller—'

'I'm saying, Mr Blair, that they're not grown much hereabouts.'

'As it happens, I've got some—not many, only about four colours. What did you want, Lindy?'

'The rather tawny ones, or something dark—'

'Would buff with a cream trumpet do? Otherwise there's yellow and salmon, purple with a white trumpet, and pink—that's all, I'm afraid. They bloom for such a short time—they're not a commercial proposition.'

'The buff and cream sound ideal, thanks, Rob. Have you got them with you?'

'No, they're growing. I'll cut them at once when I get back.'

'Can you have them delivered to me at the MacIver Hall? I'll be there from nine o'clock on.'

'Surely. How many?'

'All you've got—I've got great wide oak tubs as the base, so the arrangements have to be about three feet across.'

'Right. Would you like some astilbe, by any chance, to help fill up the frame if the columbines aren't enough? I'll bring some with me—I've got some pinkish-buff ones that you may like.'

'Thank you, Rob.' She felt his eyes dwelling on her as she noted down the colours he would supply. 'What's the matter?'

'I was just going to ask you that. Are you all right? You look a bit under the weather.'

'I'm all right, thanks. Didn't sleep very well.'

'Come and have some coffee. There's something I'd like to discuss with you.'

'Just let me put my flowers in the Mini—'

'Here, let me.' He picked up the boxes. Lindy watched while Mr Miller entered the purchases on her account, nodded to him, and followed Rob out.

They went to a little shabby 'caff' in the Canongate that opened early to cater for the market men. The coffee was very good—strong and dark, with just enough milk to take the bite off the edge. With it they had the freshly-baked rolls that are one of the early-morning treats of Scottish life.

'What was it you wanted to talk about?'

'It's a bit of an emergency. Have you ever met Mrs Margaret Warriston?'

She shook her head.

'Well, she's a florist, a very good one. She was to do the flowers for a big wedding next Saturday at St Mary's Cathedral—I've got the list here.' He produced it from his jacket pocket. 'I'm supplying the flowers . . . You see? Masses of lilies and carnations, and border pinks, and daphne. But the main thing is the gardenias—look . . .'

'Good heavens,' said Lindy, eyeing the order form. 'What's Mrs Warriston going to do with them—make a quilt?'

'As far as I understand it from the sketches, they're for the bridal headdress, and muffs. Is that right—muffs?'

'Muffs?' Lindy said, mystified. 'Oh—for the brides-maids?'

'Six of them.'

'Goodness, what a job!'

'That's the point, Lindy. Do you know how to make a muff of gardenia petals?'

'Well, yes, as a matter of fact I do.'

'And could you? Next Saturday? You see, Mrs Warriston has had to go rushing off to Argyll. Her daughter's baby has arrived a month ahead of time and there are three other children, very small I believe, that she promised to look after— Well, I won't bore you with the details, but she had to rush off last night at a moment's notice and the poor bride of next Saturday is at her wits' end.'

'Oh, poor thing! How awful! It's only five days off.'

'She can't possibly change the design of all the brides-maids' outfits at this late stage. Or at least so I gather.'

'I should think not!'

'Could you step in? Look, I've got rough sketches of the designs here. Gardenias for the muffs, with green leaves on the edges, I think. The headdress—I don't know what that's supposed to be—'

'It's a tiara shape. My word, it's complicated. That's to be gardenias and something small—I suppose it must be stephanotis. Her bouquet is lilies—that's no problem. What time is the wedding? Late afternoon, I hope! I'd have to stay up all night if it was in the morning!'

'You'll do it, then? Thanks a million, Lindy. I don't know this girl at all, but she and Mrs Warriston were both so upset . . .'

'What's her name? Madeline Spender . . . right . . .' She scribbled down the name and address. 'Will you tell her to ring me? I'll have to see her to know what the tiara is going to be attached to . . . I'll be at the MacIver Hall until about ten, and then I'm doing the flowers for the lunch tables in the hotel—let's say if she rings me after twelve o'clock.'

'That's fine. You're an absolute saviour, Lindy. Of course you'll do well out of it financially—they don't intend to spare any expense.'

She smiled. 'I'm not saying I'd take it on for nothing, but the money isn't the most important thing. The poor girl mustn't have worries like that on her great day.'

'Good, that's great. Well, I must dash—I've got a dozen boxes of carnations for the North Caledonian Hotel. See you later with the columbines and such.' With a nod he pushed his way through the crowd round the counter, a tall figure in a Fair Isle sweater and slacks. Lindy watched him go, drained her mug of coffee, then followed out to the street.

It was only as she was starting the Mini that she realised what she had done. Whether consciously or unconsciously, she had provided herself with a marvellous excuse not to go to London with Lorenz next Friday.

She went home to breakfast. When it was over, and she felt it likely that Lorenz would be up and about, she rang him. He had rooms in a flat with an Austrian couple long resident in Edinburgh—Mr Aftenwalden was a stamp dealer, rather elderly and frail, full of charm but formidable; his wife, equally elderly, ruled him with a rod of iron. Both of them had lived in Scotland so long that they spoke English with a noticeable Scottish inflection. Mrs Aftenwalden answered the call, said Lorenz was still having breakfast, in a tone that implied Lindy was very unreasonable to expect to interrupt him.

'Would you give him a message?' Lindy said. 'Tell him to do nothing about the bookings and tickets we spoke of last night. Something has come up to change my plans.'

'Bookings and tickets . . . yes.'

'Ask him to ring me after twelve.'

'After twelve . . . yes . . . very well.'

Lindy couldn't deny that she was very relieved to be spared the task of trying to explain on the phone to Lorenz. Thankfully she put down the receiver, then hurried off to the MacIver Hall.

Everything went well with the arrangements. Rob arrived with sheaves of blooms, the shapes seemed almost to construct themselves, the jars of water in the oak tubs seemed to hide themselves unbidden, the colours blended as if by magic. The table decorations were just as amenable—fifteen clusters of blue and white Star of the Veldt in little china sauceboats.

She got back home about half-past eleven. Mrs Ramsay came to the door as she drove up to say, 'Mr Hemer's rung twice, Miss Gramont. He says will you ring him as soon as you come in.'

'Very well; thank you.' She went into the hall. Just as she was about to pick up the phone, it rang. She picked it up, expecting Lorenz.

It was the bride of next Saturday, ecstatic with gratitude, eager to have her come and look at the wedding veil and the dresses, to show her the Cathedral and the containers she had agreed on with Mrs Warriston.

'Thank you, yes, this afternoon—about four? Good.

I'll see you then.' Lindy pushed down the receiver rest, then dialled Lorenz's office. It was done: she had committed herself to do the work on the wedding next Saturday. No matter what Lorenz might say now, she had given her word to Miss Spender.

As it happened, Lorenz had had to go out. His secretary had a message for Lindy: 'Would you meet him for lunch at the Tolbooth Hotel at one-fifteen, Miss Gramont?'

Lindy agreed that she would, then went to collect from her car the flowers for a silver wedding party that evening. When they had been put up to their heads in water and the containers washed and packed in the Mini, she went to change. In general she worked all through the morning in shirt and pants, but changed to a skirt or a dress in the afternoons—chiefly because the women she met in the course of her afternoon's work were well-dressed and she couldn't afford to fall below their standards.

Today she chose a crocheted dress in a colour she had privately christened 'pigeon's feather'—a sort of mauvey-grey. With it she wore a long narrow scarf of rose pink silk, grey suede shoes, and a bag to match. She looked at her hair for a long time before tying it in one thick loop at the back of her head with a piece of pink ribbon. She felt that she wouldn't disgrace the clientele of the Tolbooth, no matter how trendy they might be.

Lorenz was already there when she arrived. He rose as she was shown to the table, looking, she told herself with pride, the handsomest man in the room.

He said, smiling, 'I intended to be very angry with you, but now that I see you looking so beautiful, I find I cannot.'

'Thank you,' she said demurely.

'What did this strange message mean this morning? You told me you could arrange to be free.'

'I thought so, but now I've been asked to come to the rescue over a wedding order.' She explained briefly about Mrs Warriston and the complicated flowers that had been ordered. ' I said yes to the job before I thought what I was doing. Now that I've accepted it, I *must* do it. Poor Miss Spender would have a nervous breakdown if I backed out now.'

' *Sicherlich.* Very well, then, it does not matter so much. I shall arrange to see the Cultural Attaché at the Russian Embassy the following weekend, and we go to London Friday week instead of Friday next.'

Her heart sank like a stone. She hadn't evaded the crunch after all. ' No, Lorenz, I can't go the following weekend. I have another wedding to do that Saturday.'

' Oh, but this is a nonsense! You can't mean—'

' Saturday is my absolutely busiest day. You know that, Lorenz.'

' But you could ask some other person to take over for you.'

' No, I couldn't.'

' Why not?'

' Because I . . . I . . .'

' If this Mrs Warriston can hand over her engagements to you, then you can hand over your work to someone else.'

' But I don't *know* anyone else, Lorenz,' she said, clutching at a feeble truth. ' In London, yes—I know half a dozen girls who could take over. But here in Edinburgh—'

' From whom have you heard about Mrs Warriston and all the gardenias?'

' From Rob—Rob Blair.'

' So?' He raised his eyebrows. ' You could ask him to find someone.'

' No, I couldn't.'

' Why not?'

' Because I can't ask favours from Rob.'

Lorenz narrowed his eyes. ' This I find strange. He can ask favours from you, but you cannot ask favours from him. Why?'

' I can't explain. It goes a long way back.'

' Why do you blush when we speak of him?'

' I'm not blushing.'

' Lindy, I know my English is not perfect, but when colour comes into the face that is called a blush—not so?'

She nodded, knowing that if her face had been pink before it was scarlet now.

' Then explain why you blush when we speak of Rob.'

' It's not important—it's all finished with now.'

' Clearly it is not, if you are still so embarrassed when he is mentioned.' Lorenz leaned forward and seized her wrist. ' He was your lover?'

She pulled away from him. ' Good heavens, *no*!'

He still held her wrist, his pianist's fingers hard and strong. ' What, then? What is between you?'

' Nothing. Let me *go*.' She glanced about, lowering her voice. ' Lorenz, people are looking.'

' Let them look, it does not trouble me. What is Rob Blair to you, Lindy?'

' Let me go and I'll tell you.'

He released his grasp. She said in a dull, miserable murmur, ' We were engaged. I ran away about two weeks before the wedding. That's all.'

He frowned as he leaned towards her to catch what she said. She saw a glint of relief come into his grey-green eyes. ' You ran away?'

' Yes.'

' You didn't love him.'

' No.'

He grinned. ' I see . . . This is quite the opposite of what I was thinking!' He patted her hand. ' Come, cheer up, I'm sorry I got angry. I could not bear it if you had affection for some other man. Come, let us have a drink and we shall feel better.'

' No, Lorenz, let's finish this conversation,' she replied, summoning her courage into one strong wave that might carry her all the way to the shore. ' I think we've got important things to say to each other.'

' Indeed, what you have just told me is important.

F F—D   97

I had no idea that you had ever done such a thing!'
He shook his head. 'It puzzles me. You didn't love
him. Why did you get engaged to him?'

'Oh, need we go into all that—'

'I should like to know, Lindy.'

'Very well, I'll tell you. I'm not a bit proud of it.
My brother Arnold more or less forced me into it.'

'*Was sagst du*? You mean he told you, " You are to
marry Rob " and you agreed?'

'He didn't *tell* me, Lorenz. He just sort of made it
seem inevitable. And I only woke up to the fact that it
was a terrible mistake just before it was too late.'

'I have noticed,' Lorenz said, nodding a little, 'that
your brother is a very . . . what do you say in English
for *gebieterisch*? *Tyrannisch*?'

'Tyrannical? You can't mean tyrannical. Arnold is
autocratic, but he's a very reasonable man underneath it
all. He does tend to boss people—'

'Yes, yes—this is the word! He is bossy. He lays
down the law. It is because he is surrounded most of
the time by students. I have seen it often in university
professors.'

A few weeks ago Lindy might have allowed this verdict
to pass unchallenged; she might even have agreed with
it. But since learning to know her brother better—and
particularly since last night—she couldn't allow even
Lorenz to speak like that.

'Arnold may speak his mind forcefully. But he has
every right to. He usually speaks good sense.'

'Not when he tried to push you into marriage.'

'I keep telling you, *he* didn't say anything. It was
probably all my fault. I was too . . . too subservient.
I'm older now and I realise I could have explained my
doubts to him, and he would have understood.'

'Ah,' said Lorenz, with a rather cynical smile, 'I
would not go to a man like Arnold for advice or comfort.'

'Why not?' she cried, stung. 'We had a long talk
when I got home last night and I found him very thought-

provoking.'

'I will tell you something,' Lorenz said. 'I do not appreciate your brother very much, and I do not think he appreciates me.'

'Perhaps not. Luckily it doesn't matter very much. We're only discussing him because I was trying to explain why I can't ask Rob Blair to find a replacement for me the weekend after next.'

'Now,' he said, his tone very sharp, 'I find that silly! You say it is all in the past. Why can you not ask him?'

'I'd rather not.'

'Then ask someone else. There must be people you could ask. The firm from which you buy your flowers —they must know of other florists.'

That couldn't be gainsaid. She said: 'Yes, I expect they would. But I'm not going to ask them.'

A strange little silence ensued. Then Lorenz said: 'Why not?'

'I shan't be going to London that weekend.'

'But you said—'

'I said, when you first spoke of it, that I should love to show London to you. I thought it would be marvellous—until I understood—'

'Lindy!' he exclaimed. 'You don't have to go on! I can see what happened—it is your brother!'

'My brother?' Completely startled, all she could do was echo the word.

'He doesn't like me. I always felt this. Of course it is your brother.'

'But, Lorenz, how on earth does he come into this?'

'You told me yourself, a moment ago—you had a long talk with him last night. I see it all: He set you against me!'

'Lorenz, please—'

'What other reason? Last night you were so happy, you glowed with excitement—'

'Yes, but Lorenz, that was because I thought—'

'And then Arnold explained to you that he disapproves of me. It is quite simple. You are still afraid of your brother! You still cannot confront him!'

'No, no, darling, you've got it all wrong! It's quite true that Arnold and I had a conversation last night, but it was—'

'You talked about me, about us.'

'No, we didn't—' She broke off. 'Well, we mentioned you, but—'

'And he told you he didn't approve.'

'No, really, Lorenz—'

'You know what it is? He still wants you to marry his great friend—the good, steady, *dull* Robert Blair.'

'No, he doesn't! At least, perhaps he does, but that makes no difference—'

'Of course it makes a difference,' Lorenz said bitterly. 'This is the reason why you are still concerned about Blair. Do you think I have not seen the way you treat him? With a special gentleness, a special voice—you never speak to *me* like that!'

Lindy was beside herself. In that narrow, handsome face she could see fury, jealousy, and disappointment warring with each other so that he was almost a stranger.

Desperately she tried to clear away at least part of the misunderstanding. 'Lorenz, please believe me. My brother's feelings have nothing to do with the way I treat Rob. It just seems natural to have some special concern for him.'

'So?' Lorenz said, his voice low and tense. 'Then he attracts you still?'

The question was perhaps the last thing in the world she had expected. She was stunned by it. She looked across the table at Lorenz. The silence went on and on. He studied her with those narrowed, hard eyes.

Then he rose, and with stiff Continental courtesy gave her a little bow. 'Goodbye, Lindy,' he said, and walked away.

Some minutes later Lindy became aware that the head waiter was hovering at her elbow. He was very agitated. 'Is something wrong with the table, mademoiselle? Is m'sieur dissatisfied?'

She tilted her head to look up at him. 'No, no,' she said vaguely. 'He . . . had to leave . . . urgent business.'

'But mademoiselle will order now?'

She took the menu from him, looked blindly at it for a second or two, then handed it back.

'If you don't mind I'll . . . I would rather . . . I won't have anything.'

She got up. The head waiter, perplexed but sympathetic, moved the chair for her, gave her her handbag. 'Mademoiselle has had bad news?'

'Bad news,' she agreed, and made her way out of the restaurant.

CHAPTER VI

Luckily she had appointments that afternoon. She went to see Miss Spender, discussed the sketches for the muffs and coronet, looked at the wedding dress and veil, suggested a few alterations, then went home; but only to collect the materials for the work she had to do on the silver wedding party.

The next day and the next were much the same. She waited for Lorenz to telephone, but he did not. She debated eternally with herself: should *she* ring him? But always she decided against it. It had nothing to do with pride on her part—she would gladly have humbled herself in any way to bring about a reconciliation.

No, it was a sense of apprehension that kept her from dialling his number. If she rang him and somehow patched up their relationship, she might be repairing something that would only break down again. She felt somehow that Lorenz had to come to terms with the situation before she could resume contact with him.

She understood that the quarrel had been caused by the shock he received. First she had told him she had no intention of falling in with his plans. He had leapt to the assumption that this was due to her brother's influence. From there, jealousy had driven him to the conclusion that Rob still had some hold on her.

His view of her, at present, couldn't be in any way flattering. He saw her as weak, timid, vacillating—and perhaps even deceitful. It was true, she had never told him about Rob. She had known intuitively that he would be intensely jealous; in a situation already complicated by Marion McColl's part in his past, she had wanted to avoid the added problem of explaining Rob to him. So perhaps, to some extent, she had been deceitful.

As to being weak . . . She felt she couldn't deny this. In the past her brother *had* exerted a great influence over her. Perhaps he still did; certainly she had asked his opinion that night about love and marriage hoping for advice, however oblique, on her own problem. What he had said had gone home to her heart. Was that because he had influenced her, or because his words had supported the opinion she already had? She couldn't be sure.

Timid . . . Yes, she was timid. Instead of saying to Lorenz, when he first suggested the London weekend, 'No, I don't want to,' she had evaded the issue. She hadn't wanted a quarrel. She had grasped at a good excuse when it presented itself. Only when it became absolutely inevitable had she come out into the open and refused to go. And then, of course, he had imagined all sorts of reasons for her refusal.

Nevertheless Lorenz had to work his way through to a decision, before things could be as they used to be between them. He had to accept the fact that she, like himself, had a past which influenced her actions of the present. She was no judge of her manner to Rob, but whatever it was, she didn't intend to alter it. Nor could she altogether free herself of respect for her brother: he was her only relative, much her senior, a clever, forceful, sensible man—she could not, even for Lorenz, disregard him entirely.

What was more important, she hoped and prayed Lorenz would realise in time that these aspects of her life were unimportant. All that really mattered was their love. If it was as real to him as it was to her, in time he must come back to her ready to straighten out all the misunderstandings.

Mrs Ramsay grew very perturbed about her. 'Ye dinna eat enough to keep a spug alive, lassie,' she scolded, her tight grey curls bobbing with the vigour of her movement. 'And ye never seem to stop working. I wonder your brother allows it!'

'My brother could hardly stop me,' Lindy pointed out.

'But he's the head of the house. Forbye, you're fond

of each other—I would think you'd pay heed to him simply out of respect for family feeling.'

Lindy looked up from the accounts she was doing. ' Do you think family feeling is important, Mrs Ramsay?'

The other woman's grey eyebrows shot up. 'What'na question is that? Of course family feeling is important —you know that as well as I do myself.'

' No, I don't. You see, Arnold is really all the family I have, and there have been times when we . . . well, we weren't in contact. So I'm not very well up in family relationships.'

' Aye. Well . . .' Mrs Ramsay nodded her head two or three times, and attacked the dust on the bookshelf top with a folded cloth. 'Speaking for myself, I've two brothers and a sister, and a husband and two sons, and many a niece and nephew, and I wouldna wish them any the fewer.'

' And do you pay attention to what they think?'

' To be sure I do.'

' But if they all have different views?'

' Och, a body with sense can soon sort out the useful from the useless. The thing is, Miss Gramont, they care what I think and do, and I care what they think and do. It's awfu' comforting!'

Thinking about this afterwards, Lindy felt that Mrs Ramsay had hit on exactly the right word. It had been comforting to Lindy to know that her brother's view of life was like her own; it had made her feel less naïve, less juvenile.

Extraordinary. She would never in her life have expected Arnold to be a comfort to her.

Saturday was the great day when the Nicolson-Spender wedding was to take place. All Friday Lindy was at work in the Cathedral which, being an Episcopalian church and not Church of Scotland, was more familiar in its style than other churches where she had worked in Edinburgh. She used the materials and containers ordered for Mrs Warriston's designs but allowed her imagination free rein with them; the result was breathtaking, falling, trailing sprays of white hoya with yellow ivy and Peruvian lilies, carefully tied and supported yet appearing to float in the air. The altar flowers were pure white, the flowers at the lectern a wide fan of orange and yellow and white, the posies at the choirstall ends were gold and white.

To Lindy all these were relatively simple to do. It was the bride's and bridesmaids' flowers which were the difficulty. She spent all Friday evening making preparations and all Saturday morning at work in her hayloft; Rob delivered the gardenias and other blooms early, but like herself was too busy to do more than say 'Good morning. Good luck.'

It took her from seven-thirty in the morning until two in the afternoon, with only three breaks, one for breakfast, one for coffee, and one for a sandwich and a glass of milk. Mrs Ramsay had offered to be there to help for a couple of hours, although Saturday was not one of the days she usually came; she was a tower of strength, sewing up the finished muffs with long yet invisible stitches through the buckram, clearing away the snippings of wires, gently covering each muff with cellophane as it was finished.

The work could have been halved if the muffs had all been the same size, on florist's wire frames. But as the bridesmaids ranged in age from nineteen to five years, this was impossible; each muff had to be graded in size, and strangely enough it was the two tiniest which caused Lindy the most trouble.

When she needed a break from concentration on them, she turned to the bridal bouquet and the headdress. The coronet, though complicated, was not difficult to do; the bouquet was easier still. Each time she went back to the bridesmaids' muffs, it seemed more of a labour by comparison.

At midday Mrs Ramsay reluctantly took her leave. 'Will you manage? Can I do anything afore I go?'

'No, thanks, you've been marvellous, Mrs Ramsay.'

'You'll not forget to eat the food I've left on the tray

in the kitchen?'

'No, I promise.'

But she did forget, and to her amazement it was Arnold who brought the tray to her in the workroom. 'I'm under strict orders from Mrs Ramsay to look after you,' he observed. 'I *say*! These are somewhat splendid!'

'Do you like them?'

'Like them? Well, no—they seem a lot of work for nothing to me. But I can see they're pretty from a feminine point of view, and extremely clever.' He walked round the room, surveying her work. 'Did you do all this?'

'I did.'

'Clever girl,' he said, with a respect she had never heard in his voice before.

If he was impressed by the display in her workroom, what would he say to the total effect? 'Come to the Cathedral,' she urged.

'I should love to, my dear, I really should, but I've an appointment with Professor Dublé—I'm sorry.'

She said no more, but experienced a sense of disappointment. No one who was of importance to her was going to see her masterpiece. Well, never mind—at least she had the satisfaction of knowing her brother was pleased.

She glanced at her watch. Ten minutes to two. She had promised to deliver the bridal flowers by two-thirty, the wedding being at three-thirty. She washed hastily, combed her hair, loaded the flower-boxes into the mini-van with exquisite care, and got into the driving-seat.

The van wouldn't start. Horrified, she pressed the starter again and again. The starting motor fired, the fan whirred . . . and then died. Nothing would get the engine to turn over.

She leapt out and opened the bonnet. She had little knowledge of the internal combustion engine but enough to look at leads and connections; all seemed in good order. She checked for petrol, she checked the belt, she looked at the sparking-plugs—nothing. She made three more attempts to start, with complete lack of success.

Arnold's old estate car was gone. She ran into the house, grabbed up the telephone book, and rang the first taxi number she could find. The phone rang and rang without response—clearly all the taxis were out.

She tried four more numbers with the same result; either there was no reply or the booking-clerk told her there was no car available. 'It's Saturday, ye see,' the last one told her gently. 'A lot o' weddings and a lot o' folk going to the station and the airport for their holidays.'

'Yes, of course. Thank you.'

It was now twenty minutes past two. It would take about twenty minutes to get to Madeleine Spender's house, near the Bonaly Burn, so even supposing she were to start this very minute she was already ten minutes late with the delivery.

She rang the remaining numbers in the phone book. One firm said they had a taxi at Leith Docks delivering passengers to a cruise ship, and that they would send him as soon as he was free. She asked, 'How long?' The answer was, 'Half an hour.'

'Very well,' she said. It meant that the flowers would only get to the bride about two minutes before she left for the church, but it was better than nothing. She picked up the phone again to ring her with this warning.

It was then that inspiration struck. Rob Blair! *He* had a van, much better suited to the transport of these fragile boxes than a taxi. He might be free.

With hot and sticky fingers she dialled his number. The phone rang a long time; her heart sank. Then Rob's voice: 'Cramond 0641. Blair Nurseries.'

'Rob! Rob, thank heaven! I thought you weren't there!'

'Huh? Sorry if I didn't answer promptly—I had a mouthful of steak.'

'Oh, your lunch—of course, I'd forgotten . . . But Rob, I *do* need your help. My van's broken down.'

'Where?'

'At home. I've got all these gardenia concoctions and the bridal bouquet, and I promised to deliver by half-past two—and it's nearly that *now*!'

'Now, now,' said Rob, 'calm down. I'll be with you in fifteen minutes, with luck. So long.'

'*Thank* you, Rob!'

'Hey!'

'Yes?'

'Sit down, have a drink—you sound in a state.'

'Yes, I will—as soon as I've rung Miss Spender.'

This she did. The poor girl gave a wail of anguish, but was reassured that the flowers would be with her in about forty minutes. Next Lindy rang to cancel the taxi. Then she went upstairs, splashed her face with cold water, made herself calmly put on some lipstick, then went to the dining-room for a small brandy and large soda.

When she heard Rob draw up, she went out briskly but without panic—she was determined not to appear flustered. It was the work of seconds to transfer the boxes to his little cream van.

'You'll have to direct me. I don't know the place.'

'Straight out through Morningside. Do hurry, Rob,' she couldn't prevent herself from adding.

'Um. If we go "straight out" we'll have to negotiate Princes Street, and that's no joke on a Saturday afternoon. Okay, we'll go out to Haymarket and back —it'll be quicker, believe me. Here we go.'

It said much for his skill that, though they got mixed up in a crowd heading for an athletics meeting, they reached the Spenders' house in good time. The bride's mother greeted them at the door, resplendent in pale blue chiffon but red round the eyes from crying. Between them Lindy and Rob carried in the flowers.

'Thank you, thank you, goodbye,' said Mrs Spender, hustling them out.

Obediently they left. They got into Rob's van. All at once Lindy put her folded arms on the edge of the windscreen and dropped her head on them. She wanted to cry, she wanted to faint, she wanted to go to sleep for a hundred years, she wanted—oh, anything, anything, as a relief from the pressure.

'Here, here, what's all this?' She felt an arm go round her. 'Are you having a weep, or what?'

She made a muffled sound of denial.

'Come on now. What's the matter?' She was pulled gently upright, and then cradled against Rob's shoulder. 'Tell me all about it.'

'Nothing to tell.'

'Do you feel ill? I remember you didn't look well—'

'I'm all right.'

'Come on now, love, there must be something wrong.'

'Maybe it's just overwork.'

'Quite likely. That load we just delivered must have taken hours.'

'It did seem to go on for ever.'

'Sorry. I let you in for that—I'd no idea what was entailed.'

'No, it's all right. I enjoyed it, really—it was a challenge. It's just . . .'

'What?'

'Oh, everything's so awful.'

'Everything? That's sad.' He was stroking her hair with a light, soothing touch as he talked to her. 'Perhaps you should take on fewer commissions.'

'Oh, no, I like to be busy.'

'It's not the work, then?'

'I suppose not.'

'Arnold being troublesome?'

'No. No, as a matter of fact . . .'

'What?'

'Arnold seems nicer than he used to be.'

'Does he now? I always did think he had his good points.' He paused, but she said nothing. She didn't want to begin a discussion about Arnold. In fact, she didn't really want to do anything except stay quietly where she was, her cheek against the rough texture of the linen shirt he wore, his arm around her, the pleasantly hypnotic movement of his hand continuing across the surface of her hair.

After a few moments he said: 'If it's not the work and it's not Arnold, is it Lorenz?'

Despite herself, she stiffened.

'Ah, I see it is. What's gone wrong?'

'I don't want to talk about it.'

'That's natural enough. Do you mind if I say something, though?' She made a shrugging motion and he went on: 'I've known Lorenz longer than you. You'd probably say I don't know him so well, but at least I'm more dispassionate. Do you agree?'

She nodded.

'I don't think you should let him make you this unhappy. If you've had a quarrel, I bet it isn't nearly as important to him as it is to you.'

She sat up to look at him. 'But . . . you simply don't *know*. He was so angry!'

'I bet he got over it half an hour later.'

'Then why hasn't he been in touch?'

'That I don't know. I don't pretend to understand all the workings of his mind. Maybe he's waiting for you to make the first move.'

'Yes,' she agreed, 'but it's important that I shouldn't. Oh,' as she sensed his amusement at that, 'it's not just childish pride. I have a good reason.'

'That's your concern. All I wanted to say, Lindy, was that it's natural for someone with such a strong, fervent nature to feel things deeply, but—'

'But if Lorenz has a strong, fervent nature, how do you expect him to get over things quickly?'

Rob frowned. 'I wasn't talking about Lorenz. I was talking about you.'

'Me?'

'Yes, of course.'

'You're joking.'

'Not in the least. Why should you say so?'

'Strong? Me?'

'Yes, you—why are you so surprised?'

'But . . . but Rob! I'm anything but strong. I'm weak and cowardly—'

'Don't talk such rubbish.' He was really angry. 'Whoever told you that?'

'No one needed to tell me. I can see it in myself. I shirk every crisis. I mean . . . Rob . . . you should know that if anyone does.'

He ran a finger round the van's steering-wheel. 'You mean because you walked out on me two years ago?'

'That wasn't very brave, was it?'

'On the contrary. I thought it was extremely brave.'

'Rob!' She was truly astounded. 'You're not serious?'

'I certainly am. At the time I admit I was so hurt and angry that I couldn't see it straight. But after a bit, when I calmed down . . . Well, how many girls would have done it?'

'But, Rob—to run away without an explanation?'

'Maybe you didn't have *quite* enough courage,' he said, with a rueful grin. 'But you had a lot.'

'Oh, I can't agree—'

'Listen, Lindy, how many girls—men too—do you think have had terrible doubts and yet gone through with the marriage out of sheer lack of the courage to stand up and say, "No, it's a mistake!"? The divorce statistics probably include a lot of those. You saw you were making a mistake, and you were brave enough to do something about it.'

She said nothing. It had never occurred to her to take such a view of her own behaviour.

'Off you went to London, with no job and no training. That took a bit of doing, I imagine. Two years later, you're a success—a completely equipped artist in a very difficult profession.'

'Oh, well, perhaps, but a lot of it is instinct—'

'Most girls would have played safe—an office job or something like that. But no, you backed your own talent. And then you came here and began all over again. What's more, you didn't turn and run for it when you discovered I lived here.'

'I nearly did,' she confessed. 'I even began to pack.'

'But you unpacked again. Listen, I don't know why I should have to lecture you about your own good points. All I'm trying to say is, don't make yourself suffer unnecessarily. Get the message?'

He was studying her earnestly as he spoke, looking very directly at her so that she could see herself reflected in his bright blue eyes. Taken by a sudden impulse, she leaned forward to kiss him on the cheek.

'Thank you, Rob,' she murmured.

He coloured and drew away—whether with embarrassment or displeasure she never found out, for at that moment a motor-horn sounded an impatient challenge behind them. In Rob's wing mirrors they could see a big black limousine queueing up to get into the little driveway.

'Good lord, the first of the wedding cars!' He put the van into gear. They rolled out to the road and headed north. 'Where now?' he inquired.

'Would you mind dropping me at the Kingland Banqueting Hall in Queen Street? That's where they're holding the reception.'

'You mean you haven't finished yet?'

'Oh, I just want to check everything is okay—I did most of the arrangements yesterday. Then I *would* like to get along to the Cathedral before the ceremony is over. I'd like to see the final effect. I really have worked hard on it.' She could hear a wistful note in her voice and was ashamed of herself; good work was its own reward—to long for praise was adolescent.

In the end she reached the Cathedral while the register was being signed. She took a seat at the back, and had the pleasure of watching the procession come back down the aisle—the bride of course radiant in white wild silk and a plain tulle veil, with her headdress of gardenia and stephanotis merging perfectly. The bridesmaids were in dark blue muslin over light blue silk, so that the effect was softly iridescent; their muffs of white gardenia petals edged with violets were absolutely right. All the other flowers looked good; the total picture was of a rich yet natural beauty.

Lindy sat quietly until all the family and guests had gone. Then with a sigh of satisfaction she followed. At her elbow Rob's voice said: 'The whole thing was a work of art.'

'Rob! What are you doing here?'

'Looking at your handiwork—and my blooms! I always intended to stop by and take a look.'

'Did you? I'd no idea. Oh, I'm so glad somebody saw it!'

'Only the entire congregation, that's all.'

'No, I mean somebody that matters to me.' She took his arm in a companionable manner and they made their way towards the doors. But out on the beige-and-rose flagstones the photographers were busy so they paused to look back at the floral decor.

They began a low-pitched argument about the merits of the various blooms. So deeply engrossed were they that they didn't become aware of Lorenz until he was at their elbow.

'Good afternoon,' he said. 'Let me congratulate you, Lindy, on the success of your work.'

'Thank you.' She could hardly speak. She was conscious of an enormous surge of feeling—relief that he had come, delight in seeing him, gratitude for his having forgiven her and, she had to admit, triumph that she had won.

'Did you come on purpose to see her flowers?' Rob inquired.

'Of course. And you?' Lorenz's voice was icy.

'Oh, I grew them, so I have a vested interest. Did you see the bride and bridesmaids?'

'They are outside, being photographed.'

'Didn't you think they were rather special?'

'Very pretty.' It was quite clear he didn't care one

way or the other about the flowers, and Lindy knew he was longing for Rob to go. When he did not, but resumed his conversation with Lindy about the lasting power of the hoya he had supplied, Lorenz's mouth went hard and resentful.

Lindy was longing to tell Rob to go away. But she could scarcely do that, especially since she had been so thankful to see him there only a few moments ago; besides, he had come to her rescue, and been sweet to her when she was momentarily overwhelmed. She owed him at least politeness. So when Lorenz tried to urge her away towards a side door, she refused to move. Instead she explained to him her dilemma of an hour ago, and how Rob had saved her from disaster.

If she hoped by that to influence Lorenz's behaviour, she was sadly mistaken. If anything, his expression grew more thunderous. Watching him with apprehension, she was at a loss.

But then, praise be, Rob looked past them both towards the main door and raised his hand to beckon.

' So there you are,' he said as Marion McColl joined them. ' I thought you were going to be here for the ceremony?'

' I got held up.' She nodded a greeting at the others, her face composed and calm. ' Did it go well? Did your flowers look good, Rob?'

' Not bad. You should have seen them coming back down the aisle in a lovely cloud of gardenia fragrance. All thanks to Lindy, naturally.'

' Nonsense. If you hadn't provided the flowers—'

' Let's say it was a joint effort. How's the crowd outside, Marion? Can we get out that way?'

' Oh yes, you just go round the edge.'

' Marion and I agreed to meet here and then go and have tea in the Gardens. Coming?'

' No, thank you,' said Lorenz. ' Lindy and I have other plans.'

This was news to Lindy, but she was perfectly happy with the arrangement. She went with him to his car;

without consulting her he set off at a brisk pace west-ward. As the houses thinned out she said: 'Where are we going?'

'I have no idea. Here is yet another of these innu-merable golf courses. We can perhaps get out and walk there—is that permitted?'

'I'm sure it is. Look, that's a footpath we just passed.'

'*Schön.*' He slowed, stopped, backed to the spot she had pointed to, and parked. They took the path off to the right which, had they but known it, was called Lover Loan. Lorenz walked fast, so that she could hardly keep up with him.

'Lorenz,' she said at last breathlessly, 'is this a race?'

He slowed his pace. 'You didn't seem surprised to see me in the Cathedral just now.'

'Didn't I?'

'Were you surprised?'

'Indeed I was.'

'You didn't seem very pleased either.'

'Perhaps I'm too tired to show much reaction.'

'In fact,' he said, ignoring her words, 'you seemed more interested in Rob than in me.'

She shook her head.

'You deny it? Yet you went on talking to him.'

'What did you expect me to do—turn my back on him? That wouldn't be polite. Besides, he had just done me a great favour.'

Lorenz seized her by the shoulders. 'You told me you could not ask a favour from him!'

'This favour wasn't for myself.'

'For whom, then?'

'Lorenz,' she said, surprised at the crispness of her own manner, 'I won't be cross-questioned.'

He didn't catch the phrase; he looked at her, still indignant, but puzzled both at the word and the way she uttered it.

'I don't think I owe you an explanation if I'm polite to someone,' she went on. 'If you came to the Cathedral this afternoon simply to quarrel with me again, you could have spared yourself the trouble.'

'I came to talk to you—to say I was sorry. And I find you with that man!'

'Heavens above, can't you see how absurd you're being? He went off with Marion, didn't he?'

'I do not say *he* cares for *you* any more. I say that *you* care for *him*.'

She took time before she replied. 'I do care for him,' she admitted. 'I didn't expect to say that, but it's true. I used to be very fond of him in the past, and now that I've got to know him again I'm still fond of him. But I don't feel about him the way I do about you, Lorenz.'

He drew her towards him, smiling, mollified by the gentleness of her words. 'How do you feel about me, my darling?'

'I love you, Lorenz. You know that.'

'And I love you.'

When they kissed, it was almost as if the quarrel between them had never happened.

Almost. Not quite.

CHAPTER VII

It seemed that Lorenz could never quite forget that Cindy had once been on the verge of marriage with another man. Although she did all she could to reassure him—spent every moment with him, rang him when she was on an assignment, took up the habit of writing to him every day however briefly—nothing was quite enough.

She would feel everything was going well; then some tiny episode would alert her. One day, for instance, Lorenz said àpropos of nothing: 'Why do you wear so often the colour green?'

'Do I?' she queried, surprised and mentally reviewing her wardrobe.

'Yes, often. You know I do not like green.'

'No, I didn't know that, Lorenz.'

'But last time you wore green I told you.'

She searched her memory. It had been an emerald green skinny sweater. 'Oh, that! I thought it was the sweater you didn't like.'

'I suppose,' Lorenz said through his teeth, '*someone else* likes you in green.'

At moments like that she never knew whether to have it out or to ignore it. This time she chose to say in a neutral tone, 'I've never asked anyone what they think of the colours I wear—except Julia, my friend in London.'

From then on she tried to wear the outfits about which Lorenz had expressed approval, to do her hair the way he preferred, to use eye make-up but not lipstick since he said she looked best that way. But it was a dubious solution, because one afternoon, headed for a business appointment where she wanted to make a good impression, she put on a green dress and piled her thick chestnut hair on top of her head for coolness.

The business talk went well. One of the guests at the

Nicolson-Spender wedding had observed the flowers been impressed, and was now offering her a plum job. At the opening of the Edinburgh Festival at the end of August, a group of South American businessmen would be present; they had loaned art treasures from their own collections for a special exhibition. They had taken over for the time of their stay a small but very select hotel in Queen Street—and the owner, John Urquhart, was now asking Lindy to provide all the flowers for the hotel throughout their stay of six days.

'It will be quite a task,' he warned. 'I have twenty bedrooms, six public rooms including the ballroom, and various vestibules and foyers. I want flowers in all of them—even the bathrooms, if you can think of anything that would suit!'

She laughed. 'Don't worry, Mr Urquhart. I can do it.'

'The important thing is the last day. The bankers of the city are giving a banquet for them here in the ballroom. I want something particularly special that evening—I want to create a really tremendous effect if I can. Their wives are accompanying some of them, you see—I want the ladies to feel that the hotel appreciates the honour.'

'May I see the ballroom?'

'Surely. This way.' She followed Mr Urquhart's broad rugby-player's back down from his private suite at the top to the ballroom on the ground floor. It was a superbly proportioned room: not as big as the ballroom of a commercially-designed hotel but reflecting the perfect taste of the eighteenth-century architects who had built this part of Edinburgh.

What particularly appealed to Lindy was the colour scheme. The walls were covered in ivory figured silk; when she went close to it she discovered that the design of the weave was tiny garlands of narcissus. The ceiling, quartered by richly ornamented mouldings painted white, was a warm terra-cotta. The heavy tapestry curtains draped at the tall sash windows were the same

lour; the only other tint in the room was the gold
hich picked out some of the moulding.

Into her mind came a picture of the orchid blossoms
Rob Blair's greenhouse—the dark red and cream
owers massed on their slender, flexible stems, the shade
f the petals a little darker than the terra-cotta and ivory
f the decor here . . .

'I know just the thing for this room,' she announced.
An orchid—'

'Orchids? Oh, I'm not keen on those big purple
ings, Miss Gramont.'

'You mean cattleya. No, I wasn't thinking of using
ose. This is a smaller bloom in just the right colour
-and it's never been used before for floral decoration.
friend of mine has just produced it from a cross
etween some other orchids; I don't know much about
e growing of it, but I can assure you, the minute I
w it I asked if he would save it for me for a special
casion.'

Urquhart's ruddy complexion gained even more colour
he blushed with pleasure. 'Well, I must say, that
unds good. Let me show you what I have in mind for
e table arrangement.' They paced about while he set
indly gilt chairs to simulate the layout, described
lverware and china and linen, showed her the planned
enu. There were to be five South Americans and their
omenfolk, either wives or daughters; five bankers and
eir wives; representatives from the Scottish National
allery, the Arts Council, merchants of the city, in all
inging the guest list to forty.

'Can you deal with it?'

'Yes, I'm sure I can. I won't accept any work for
couple of days before. Which day of the week is the
anquet?'

'The Tuesday. They arrive on the Friday. On the
aturday they're the guests of the Provost and Corpora-
on for various events, ending with the midnight Tattoo
t the Castle—pray for a fine night! Sunday they go to
e service for the opening of the Festival and get shown

round Holyrood. Monday they attend the opening of the art exhibition and so on. Tuesday we give them a day to themselves, which means the ladies will head straight for Princes Street to buy Scottish knitwear. That evening we give them the banquet as a send-off. Does that fit in for you?'

'Perfect. It means I can be in and out of the hotel most days while they aren't here, to see to the flowers, and Tuesday I can have the ballroom all day, I take it?'

'Surely.' He gave her a broad smile. 'I'm going to have photographs taken, Miss Gramont. The publicity value will be enormous.'

They talked over the cost, tea was served to them in a Georgian silver pot, they shook hands, and she left. She was tense with excitement; what an opportunity! A job like this might so easily have gone to one of the big organisations—to be offered to a freelance was a great compliment.

She went at once to Rob's nurseries. He was engaged with a trio of student helpers in taking out old plants from one of the open air beds, but scrambled to his feet as she drove in.

'Lindy! What a pleasant surprise. Forgive the grime—' he dusted himself off with his hands—'but while I've got extra people during the summer holidays, I like to get things going.'

'Rob,' she said, pulling him by the shirtsleeve, 'show me that orchid!'

'Which—? Oh, the new one?' He went with her as she hurried to the orchid house. With accustomed care he opened the door, showed her in, and closed the door behind them.

The pots with the deep red orchid were on a shelf at eye level. Cascading down from it came this torrent of winged blossoms; as they approached Lindy was aware of a faint scent, a woody fragrance which she couldn't identify.

'Oh, it's so beautiful—like a fleet of little fairy boats! I do love it, Rob!'

'It's odd you should notice the boat-shape. Its name, cymbidium, comes from the Greek word meaning boat. I'm glad you still like it. All the same,' he added, adjusting a screen to let in more light, 'you didn't come here just to be told its Greek name. To what do I owe the honour?'

'Rob, I've got the most *fabulous* commission. The Darrin Hotel—five millionaires from Argentina or somewhere—a banquet with all sorts of important people—'

'Hi, hi, slow down You're talking like a telegram. What five millionaires?'

More sensibly she explained the project. He listened with growing interest. 'My word! Next thing is, you'll be asked to go to Argentina to do work for them there. Sounds great. And you want my new cymbidium?'

'May I, Rob? It means every single bloom you have here, I think.'

'They're yours. They always were.'

'Thank you. I'm tremendously grateful. As to price, Mr Urquhart is prepared to pay anything you care to ask.'

'Don't tempt me! You mean "anything in the price range for orchids", of course.'

'He's aware this is a new variety. You can take that very much into account.'

Rob laughed. 'I must say you've been good for business, Lindy. Don't you think we ought to make a proper arrangement whereby I pay you a percentage commission on big orders like this?'

'Oh, goodness . . . what an idea! I'm just glad to be able to get flowers of this calibre. I honestly never thought I would, so far from the main market in London. Really *I* should pay *you* commission!'

'How about a partnership? Exclusive rights to the best blooms in my greenhouses—you'd be unbeatable.'

Chuckling, she shook her head. 'I'm not expecting to be here much longer, thanks.'

'Not—?' He turned quickly to look at her. 'Why not?'

'I only decided to stay until after the Festival, you know.'

'No, I didn't know that.' He seemed to consider his next words carefully before uttering them. 'Do I gather from that that Lorenz will be leaving Edinburgh after the Festival?'

'It seems likely. He'd rather work on the Continent, I think. At the moment there's a chance of a job in Salzburg.'

'I see.'

The youngster who was on the permanent staff appeared at the greenhouse door. 'Mr Blair—telephone.'

'Thank you, Alec.' Rob motioned to Lindy. 'If you've seen all you want to, we may as well go when the door's open—no point in opening and closing it unnecessarily.'

'Yes, of course.' They followed the boy towards the house. Lindy said goodbye and walked towards her Mini. Despite attention after its breakdown it was still being temperamental, so she was gentling it round to take her departure when she became aware that Rob had come out and was waving to her. She stopped. He came up to her window, frowning.

'That was Lorenz,' he told her.

'Lorenz?'

'He asked if you were here. I said you had just left —I thought you had.'

It was Lindy's turn to frown. 'What did he want?'

'He didn't say.'

They gazed at each other.

'What an odd thing,' she murmured. 'How could he possibly have known I was here?'

'You told him, I expect.'

'No, I didn't know until I left the Darrin Hotel . . .' It was beyond her. 'Never mind, I'm seeing him this evening, so whatever it was, he can tell me then.'

She drove off, still rather perplexed but dismissing it from her mind. Only that evening did she learn the extent of the problem. She was dining with Lorenz at the Aftenwaldens' flat so that, until the two old people left them alone after the meal, she noticed nothing amiss. But as soon as they had gone, Lorenz began the attack.

'You went to see Rob Blair this afternoon!'

'Yes, I did. And you rang me. I was still there, as a matter of fact—'

'He told me you had gone!'

'I was in my van. He came out to tell me just as I drove off. I did wonder how you—'

'You did not ring me back.'

'Well, no, since we were meeting this evening—'

'You did not really wish that I should know you had gone there.'

'Don't be silly, Lorenz. It wasn't a secret—'

'You did not tell me you were going.'

'No, because I didn't know myself. It was only after—'

'That is a lie! I *saw* you—in Queen Street. You were wearing a dress he likes and the hair in a crown and—'

'Lorenz!' she exclaimed. 'Lorenz, what are you saying?' She stared at his tormented face. 'You can't really imagine I dressed up specially to go and dazzle Rob?'

'This afternoon you did not look as you do now.'

She glanced down at the cream cotton dress with its girlish pattern of rosebuds. It was a demure Victorian style that Lorenz particularly loved, and to go with it she had her hair tied back in a simple Mozart bow of cream satin. She would not have gone to a business interview in anything so romantic and *jeune fille*; instead she had worn something rather crisp and business-like, and the fact that it happened to be a dress Lorenz didn't like was neither here nor there, since she hadn't expected to see him.

'This afternoon, darling, I was going to talk to the manager of the Darrin Hotel—'

'Yes, but afterwards you were going to see Rob. Why else do you wear the clothes he likes?'

'Oh, Lorenz, don't be absurd!' she burst out, thoroughly exasperated. 'Englishmen don't give a hang what women wear—Scotsmen even less, I imagine. I have no idea what is Rob's favourite colour or whether he notices how I do my hair—most likely not. And even if he did, I wouldn't bother. I don't consult him.'

'But the moment you receive this commission from the hotel, you rush off to tell Rob. You do not rush to me.'

She drew in a breath and let it go in a sharp sigh. 'If you could supply me with the flowers I need for the Darrin Hotel, then I'd rush to you.'

'He is important to you, then. More than me.'

'Stop it, Lorenz!' She got up. 'One more word, and I'm going.'

'Lindy—'

'I mean it. I hate this stupid behaviour.'

He grasped her hands. 'I won't say any more. Only promise me, Lindy—promise not to see him.'

'No,' she said, shaking her head emphatically, 'I can't do that. I need Rob—'

'*Need* him?'

'For the flowers he grows. Oh, Lorenz, stop putting a wrong construction on everything I say!'

'These flowers, I hate them. I wish you did not do this work, then there would be no need to see him.'

'I couldn't avoid it even then. Rob's a friend of my brother's.'

'You see? First you give me one excuse and then you give another—'

'Right, that settles it. I'm going.'

'Lindy!'

'Goodnight, Lorenz.'

'No, no, don't go, Lindy, I won't say any more. Stay, Lindy, please stay.'

And because he was contrite, and she truly believed this stand she had made would bring him to his senses, she gave in.

In the city the tempo of life accelerated. As August

came visitors poured in, and also the performers for the main events of the Festival and the enthusiasts who would make up the Fringe. Church halls, school gymnasiums, lecture rooms, warehouses—anything that could house an audience was hired for some group of hopefuls.

Marion McColl was busy arranging and rehearsing her programmes for the Fringe concerts. She was to give four piano recitals, in what was now the entrance hall of a tweed merchant in Forth Street but had once been the vestibule of an Adam brothers' house. Lindy saw her from time to time: they still foregathered, Arnold's friends, at the Sunday rendezvous at Gullane when they could manage it, although as the Festival came closer most of them had commitments of some kind. Lindy learned that almost the entire population of Edinburgh seemed to get involved; they took part in the performances, they helped with scenery or programme-selling or ushering, they offered hospitality, acted as guides, organized parties, and in general threw themselves into the event with total zest. Even the crews on the buses and the waitresses in the tea-shops were 'Festival-minded', prepared to give directions to strangers and attempt conversations in any of a score of languages.

As a respite, it was sometimes necessary to get away. So on Sundays Lindy and Lorenz would head for the countryside so close on Edinburgh's doorstep, sometimes to the Hundergate Hotel, sometimes to the dig at Braco.

They were gathered round their usual group of tables at the Hundergate on the Sunday before the beginning of the Festival. A great argument had been raging about what to do a week from today—should they all go to the service in St Giles for the opening of the Festival?

'If this fine weather holds the Cathedral will be crammed,' Hamish objected. 'It was, last year.'

'Moreover it's a waste to go indoors in weather like this.' That was John Dennison.

'I vote we go to Braco and do something useful,' Arnold said.

125

'Useful? You say that as if we haven't all been slaving away for weeks at something " useful "!'

'Besides,' Lorenz put in, glancing at Marion, 'you ought not to risk any cuts to your hands. Your first recital is on Monday week.'

She nodded agreement, a glow of gratitude quickly hooded behind dropped eyelids. 'But I do want to get out of town next Sunday for a bit,' she ventured. 'I know I'll be terribly keyed up if I just stooge around.'

'I'll tell you what,' Rob suggested. 'We'll all get up early and go out to the hills. A bit of exercise, a picnic lunch, and then home to my place for a serve-yourself supper—how's that?'

Cries of 'Marvellous' 'What a great idea!' greeted this plan. Lindy glanced rather anxiously at Lorenz, but he seemed to have no objection. The idea was approved; they adjourned to lunch.

The intervening week was hectically busy for everyone except perhaps Arnold. Lorenz was checking and finalising all the transport and accommodation he had arranged for the visiting musicians; Marion was practising, practising, practising; Rob was working from dawn to dusk on flowers ordered for Festival decorations. As for Lindy, she had so much to do that she needed forty-eight hours to each day.

On the Thursday she went to the Darrin Hotel with the Mini full of blossoms and foliage and florist's aids. Containers were being supplied by George Urquhart for the most part, but she had brought some of the curios unearthed when she and Mrs Ramsay cleared the hayloft; she knew the ladies from South America would love them.

She had decided to use mainly simple flowers for the daily arrangements—English flowers, Scottish flowers—because she felt that the more exotic blossoms would be quite well known to them; many of the expensive flowers beloved by florists actually originated in South America. So instead she used many blooms of the daisy type—asters, ox-eyes, marguerites—and many wild varieties too which she picked on the Pentland Hills, such as corn marigolds and ragwort. She picked, too, delicate bunches of the Scots bluebell, which the English call the harebell, the single bell flowers nodding on their slender stems.

The effect she achieved was light and cool, except for two lush conversation pieces in the foyer, which she arranged like an old Dutch flower painting. Mr Urquhart was delighted, and reported to her by telephone on Friday evening that the women guests had already commented on the flowers.

On Saturday morning, just to show that she could do it more than once, she went to the hotel at break of day and changed all the arrangements in the public rooms, using pansies and violets and petunias and hydrangeas and dahlias. It was a virtuoso performance; as she drove off she gave a little grin of satisfaction. She wanted the guests to notice the trouble she had taken so that, on the night of the banquet, they would come into the ballroom looking expectantly to see what she had done. Sunday morning, again, she renewed the flowers, using white as her colour theme, and leaving a little corsage of white violets for each of the ladies to wear to the Cathedral ceremony.

That done, she went home to eat a hasty breakfast before Lorenz arrived to drive her to the hills. She had been given a map on the previous evening with their route pencilled in: across the Forth by the new bridge, west through the Ochils to Menstrie, just north of which village they would see the group waiting.

When they arrived it was about ten o'clock on a morning of cloudy sunshine, very mild but with a pleasant wind blowing down the valley. A long aspect of rising ground, brilliantly green but speckled with the dark of gorse, led the eye up to a rounded peak.

'That looks imposing,' Lindy commented. 'What's it called?'

'That's Dumyat,' Rob told her, 'about thirteen hundred feet. That's where we're going.'

'Up there?' She looked apprehensively at the rough track sloping upwards towards the shoulders of the hill.

'Why not? A great day for walking. Your shoes are okay, are they?' He surveyed them. 'Yes, you're all set. How about you, Lorenz?'

'My shoes are good,' Lorenz said coldly.

'Fine. Will you take this rucksack? Lindy, perhaps you'd carry this basket—look after it, the wine is in it! Okay, everybody ready? Off we go!'

When, last Sunday, he had recommended 'a bit of exercise', Lindy had had no idea he really meant an excursion of this kind. It was strenuous walking, the slope steep and the surface of the track very uneven. Luckily the higher they went, the stronger the breeze; and they stopped often to rest and admire the view.

They struggled up to the summit of Dumyat in good time to find a pleasant corrie for lunch. Rucksacks were thankfully thrown down and unpacked, food was laid out, the wine was put in a nearby burn to cool. There were fresh rolls and butter, chicken, tongue and cheese, washed down with what Arnold described as 'vinum ordinarium', a cheap Spanish Sauternes. Afterwards they lolled about in the sunshine. Lindy spied a pair of curlews who occupied her attention for the next half hour or so.

Then, feeling that as she was fifty yards or so from the peak of Dumyat she might as well admire the view, she got up and rather laboriously walked to the top.

The outlook was very pleasing. To the east she could see a range of hills, with water glinting beyond—she took this to be the Firth of Forth. To the north were mountains whose names were unknown to her, but they were clearly the beginnings of the true Highlands. Immediately to the west was a wide expanse of turf and stone; she thought she had heard this mentioned as the Great Glen, separating the peak from the western top of Dumyat.

As she stood idly watching, she realised that figures were moving about on the slope below her. After a moment she recognised one by the bright red hair—it was Hamish.

Her brother came to join her at her viewpoint. 'Watching the climb?' he inquired.

'What climb?'

'It's Hamish and Rob on some piece of rock. Energetic pair, aren't they?'

'Can we go and watch from nearby?'

'If you want to. You'd better put a snap in it, though, or they'll be finished before you get there.'

'How do I get there?'

'Back down to the picnic area and then round the shoulder of the hill.'

They retraced their steps. Lorenz got up as they approached. 'Where have you been?'

'Looking at the view. Now I'm going to look at the climbers—on the rock face in the gully.'

He shrugged. 'I didn't know you were interested in climbing.'

'I'm not really, but this happens to be Hamish and Rob. I thought I'd like to see them in action.'

'I will come with you,' he said quickly.

'I'll come too,' Marion put in, scrambling to her feet to follow Lorenz.

They trudged round the slope and over the slippery grass to skirt some very loose boulders and cross a terrace of grass and gravelly scree. Here they found a pinnacle of rock growing out of the hill close to the rock face so that it formed a climber's chimney a little over thirty feet high.

Hamish was on top of the cliff, half sitting, half kneeling, with a coil of rope in his hands. The rope went down over the rock. Lindy couldn't see where it ended for a moment, then out of the shadow between the pinnacle and the rock-wall a figure emerged—Rob, about halfway up.

'Hi,' Hamish announced, 'you've got an audience.'

'A what?'

'An audience.'

F F—E   129

Rob peered up, shading his eyes.

'Not here, below you.'

He leaned over to look down. Lindy's heart came into her mouth. But all that happened was that he shifted his weight from one foot to the other and said casually, 'Oh, hello. I thought you were all having a snooze.'

'What a strange chap you are,' said Arnold. 'How can you possibly enjoy clambering about like a mountain goat?'

'We're not all as old and infirm as you,' Rob replied. He looked up. 'How'm I doing, Hamish?'

'You shouldn't have changed weight just then. Your next move is with the foot you're standing on.'

'We're distracting him,' Lindy murmured to the others. 'Let's move away.'

'Oh, there is nothing difficult in what he is doing,' said Lorenz. 'It is only a short climb.'

'Short or long, if he falls he'll hurt himself.'

'But he will not fall. He is roped up.'

'Where did you find the next hold?' Rob called up. 'You didn't cross this slab, did you?'

'No, my reach is too short. You could do it, though—'

'Yes, to that triangle crevice. All right, hold on, here I go.' Rob seemed to reach out round the side of the rock-tower, hang in space, and then move upward. Lindy gasped in horror, and then gave a little laugh of relief when he moved on without effort.

'It looks so dangerous,' she said.

'Dangerous—how can it be dangerous when he is roped and only a few feet from the ground?' said Lorenz. 'And on this little hill—a nothing! In my homeland we have real mountains—the Gross Glockner is ten times as high as this.'

For the first time since they reached the grassy terrace where the climb began, Lindy looked at Lorenz; until now all her attention had been on Rob. She saw, to her dismay, that Lorenz was watching the man on the

130

liff face with his mouth pulled down in resentment and
lislike. It came back to her with wounding force that,
lespite all she could say and do, Lorenz was still jealous.
She was at a loss what to say. Luckily Arnold spoke
up.

'Did you do any climbing in Austria, Lorenz?'

'Of course. Much more than *this*.'

'They only do these little short climbs for practice,'
Marion put in. 'There are some very long and difficult
rock-faces in the Highlands, especially on some of the
north sides of the mountains—'

'You know all about it, it seems,' Arnold teased.

'Oh, Rob has been talking to me about it. He's
promised to take me next time he goes.'

'Won't that be a bit dull for you? Since you yourself
don't climb?'

'Well,' Marion said, with a flashing glance at Lindy,
'I've nothing else to do with my spare time these days.'
She forced a little laugh. 'I daresay I'll find something
to do in Skye while Rob is tackling the Cuillins.'

'Coolings?' Lorenz echoed. 'In the sky?'

'Cuillins, darling. A mountain group on the island of
Skye—only small compared with your Tyrolean mountains.' Lindy took his arm, turning away from the climb
so that he would see she was giving her attention to him
and by her tone tried to convey that to her he was the
important person. Yet even as she did so she was conscious of a weariness at having to adapt her behaviour
to keep Lorenz happy. Her real interest at the moment
was in how Rob was getting on.

A sudden shout made her jerk her head round. A
piece of shale came ricocheting down between the pinnacle and the rock face—the shout from Rob had been
warning to those below, not alarm for himself.

'What're you doing, staging an avalanche?' Hamish
called down.

'All jolly fine for you, sitting up there in the breeze.
I'm all hot and sticky.' Rob paused to peer down at
his audience. 'Nobody got hit, I take it?'

'No, we're all right,' Arnold reported, cupping his hands to his mouth.

'Just keep away where you are, will you? I'm at the tricky part now and this stuff isn't called pudding-stone for nothing—it's pretty rotten.'

Lindy was longing to call, 'Be careful, Rob,' but bit her lip to keep back the words. Lorenz, quite uninter-ested, was now making his way along the grass hillside back to the gully which would lead him round to their picnic site. She lingered a moment, twisting her head to see Rob make another move upward, but then Lorenz stopped to look back in obvious impatience; she hurried to join him.

Later, through the field-glasses brought by one of the other girls, she was able to watch Rob join Hamish in safety at the top of the rock chimney. She sighed in relief. As she walked back from her viewpoint Lorenz said, 'What were you looking at?'

'A curlew,' she replied at once, without stopping to think. And then was horrified—she had been reduced to lying, simply to avoid irritating Lorenz.

Once the group was reassembled, they began the walk back to the cars. Going down was much easier than going up, so it was still not yet six o'clock when they piled into their transport to head for Rob's place. Since neither Lindy nor Lorenz knew the route, Hamish volun-teered to go as a passenger in Lorenz's car. Lindy there-fore found herself in the back seat where she was joined, somewhat to her surprise, by Marion.

There was very little conversation on the drive. Hamish was the most talkative of the quartet, discoursing with enthusiasm about Rob's talent as a climber. Lorenz made almost no response and Lindy took care not to do so unless Hamish spoke to her directly. All the while she could feel Marion's curious glance resting on her, cool and unfriendly.

When they reached Cramond Brig, the sky had cleared of its cloud due to the breeze which had been freshening all day from the north. It was chill and crisp as they tumbled out of the cars. The girls were directed to the upstairs bathroom to freshen up before the meal, while the men were given the freedom of the workmen's shed where the water taps and equipment for hosing the greenhouses were kept.

When Lindy came downstairs again, Rob was explaining that it would take another ten or fifteen minutes for the food to heat up. 'Scotch broth in the soup-pot, Scotch mutton pies in the oven, and Gaelic coffee to follow—but it all needs to be piping hot. So if you'd like to wander out and look at the plants, feel free.' He caught sight of Lindy as she joined the group. 'Want to come and look at your orchid?' he invited.

'May I?'

'Come along.' One or two others tacked themselves on. He led a little crowd of six people to the orchid house, including not only Lindy, but Marion and Lorenz.

'What does he mean, "your" orchid?' Lorenz demanded as they walked across the gravel.

'Oh, it's just . . . it's an orchid I'm going to use for a tremendously important piece of floristry on Tuesday.'

'What kind of floristry?' Marion asked, staying close to Lorenz on the other side.

'There's a big banquet—at least, not big in numbers but terribly important people—'

'It's the South American millionaires,' put in Rob, catching the gist of the conversation. 'Just a minute, everybody.' He drew them to a halt outside the door. 'Would you all mind coming in without too much flapping and moving about? Orchids don't like draughts or currents of cold air, and as you've probably noticed by now, it's pretty fresh out of doors now.'

He eased open the door. They all filed in obediently. He closed the door behind him. In contrast to the air outside, the seventy-degrees temperature and the humidity struck like a gauze curtain against the cheeks.

'Phew, I shouldn't like to work in here!' Hamish remarked. 'Do you mean to say that orchids enjoy this?'

'They certainly do. Cymbidium, especially, likes a nice moist spray on its leaves in really hot weather, to keep it happy. And when I'm sowing seed, the bottles have to be kept in an atmosphere even damper than this, believe me.' He moved round the walks, pointing out good specimens and giving information when asked. 'They are, of course, all very delicate—a breath of frost could do them all in.'

'Which is the orchid Lindy was talking about?' Lorena inquired.

'Here it is.' He turned the group to look at the special bay in which the shelves were housed. There were exclamations of delight, especially from the girls, at the falling curtain of dark-red and cream blooms. 'Not bad, is it? I'm going to have pictures taken— at least, Mr Urquhart of the Darrin Hotel is having them taken—and then I'll send some to the *Orchid Review* with a few details.'

'You mean it's something new?' asked Marion.

'Yes, a new variety—Lindy is having the first public appearance for her banquet decoration.'

'I'm terribly grateful,' she put in. 'I've found a little pillar of polished dark grey marble and a pewter urn—the whole thing is going to look superb . . . at least I hope so.'

'You should think yourself jolly lucky,' said Marion. 'Rob doesn't let just anyone have his plants.' She quite obviously wanted to impress on the others the fact that she, Marion, had some sort of proprietorial rights over this extraordinary man who could produce this new and rare flower.

Lindy, understanding her feelings, played up to them. 'Oh, I do, I assure you. After all, these people from Argentina and Brazil are used to the best, so I had to have something extra-special for this dinner. I've got it all planned out and made some sketches. First thing Tuesday morning I shall set to work in the ballroom at the Darrin Hotel, and the result—I hope!—will be a masterpiece.'

'Fancy!' murmured Sheila Davison. 'It's quite like a theatrical first night, isn't it? "Dinner at the Darrin", starring—What's the name of the orchid, Rob?'

'It hasn't got a name if it's all that new,' Hamish suggested.

'Oh yes, it has. I gave it a name a couple of months ago—it's cymbidium "Doralinda".'

Lindy's head lifted sharply at the words. She met his eyes and felt herself going scarlet with surprise and pleasure. That was *her* name, the name forgotten in favour of the diminutive her mother used to use, Lindy.

Most of the others failed to guess the connection. But she heard Lorenz give a little exclamation of irritation, and she saw Marion dart a glance at her and then at the orchids. But why should it perturb them so? Rob had named the flower for her because she was to have the privilege of using it first, that was all. Why should both Lorenz and Marion be so determined to take exception at every example of friendship between herself and Rob?

Sadly she had to admit that perhaps, from Marion's point of view, there might be justification. Marion had lost Lorenz to her but then had been lucky enough to gain friendship and affection—perhaps more—from Rob. To learn that he had sufficient feeling for Lindy to dedicate the orchid to her—that must be bitter indeed!

All evening Lindy tried to find occasions to show Marion a special consideration, but in the noisy, chattering group it wasn't easy. Nor would Lorenz let her move far from his side. She was glad when she was able to say it was time to go, on the grounds that she had to be up early for the flower market.

As she was taking leave she managed to have a word aside with Rob. 'Thank you, Rob. About the orchid.'

'Think nothing of it—I just felt it was appropriate.'

'I'm very flattered.' She took his hand, pressed it, and joined Lorenz in the doorway.

In almost total silence he drove her home. He made no move to get out at her door. 'Aren't you coming in for a drink or something?' she invited.

'Oh, I think not, since you have to be up so early to go to fetch your precious flowers.'

'Lorenz, what *is* the matter?'

'Nothing. I have had a most agreeable day. First you show a lot of worry when Rob shows off at some little piece of climbing, and then you blush like a schoolgirl when he tells you his new orchid is named for you. And last of all you hold hands when you say goodnight. I wonder you did not throw your arms round him and kiss him!'

She drew a slow, deep breath. What was the use? She had tried so hard today—she had even told a white lie to placate him. And all the same he was consumed with foolish jealousy.

'I was worried,' she agreed. 'I know nothing about rock-climbing—it looked dangerous to me.'

'You were only worried because *he* was climbing.'

'No, Lorenz. I'd have been just as worried if Hamish had been on that rock face.'

'And would you have held *his* hand so long when it was time to go?'

'Believe what you like!' she cried, her patience snapping. She turned, went indoors, and slammed the door shut after her. She stood there for a while, shaking with anger and distress, leaning against the inside of the panels. She half hoped, half dreaded that he would call to her; but after a moment she heard him drive off.

She went to bed half expecting not to sleep. But the fresh air and the day's exertions and the lateness of the hour combined to act as a drug, and before long she was dead to the world.

As usual her alarm woke her. She was up and out in half an hour, spent an hour at market, went straight to the Darrin Hotel to do the flowers in the rooms for today, Monday, and got home to find Arnold yawning and in his dressing-gown, boiling the kettle for his early morning tea.

'Umm . . . Good morning,' he mumbled. 'What's it

136

like outside?'

'A bit nippy, so far. Here, let me . . .' She took over the tea-making. 'What time did you get home?'

''Bout one o'clock. I'd have been even later except that someone else took Marion home. Did you enjoy yesterday?'

'I liked the view from the top of Dumyat.'

'That's what's called "damning with faint praise", I believe. I agree it was a day of mixed blessings.' He searched in the pockets of his dressing-gown for his glasses, then put them on to study her. 'Lorenz give you a bad time?'

She shrugged. 'We had words.'

'I could feel it in the air. He really is temperamental, Lindy.'

'So is Marion. Maybe it's to do with being musicians or something.'

'Yes, Marion was in a bit of a state too—one could sense it. What was it all about?'

'Oh, it isn't worth discussing.' She fetched cups and saucers from the dresser, carefully stepping over little Meg Merrilies as she did so. She was just pouring fresh milk into a saucer, accompanied by ecstatic purring from the little cat, when the phone rang.

She straightened. 'So early?' she murmured.

Arnold took the milk bottle from her. 'I believe the phone wakened me about a quarter of an hour ago, now I come to think of it.' He bent to finish providing Meg Merrilies' breakfast.

Lindy went out to the phone. 'Lindy Gramont here,' she announced.

'Lindy?' It was Rob. 'Lindy, something awful's happened.'

'What?' Frightening visions raced through her mind —accidents, quarrels, accusations, physical mishaps. 'What is it, Rob?'

'The orchid—it's ruined.'

'*What?* What do you mean, ruined?'

'Come and see. I'm sorry, Lindy, you won't be able

137

to use any of them—there was a sharp north wind last night and somehow the door of the greenhouse got left open.'

She said she would be there within half an hour. She knew, even before she put the phone down, that the greenhouse door had not opened by accident.

CHAPTER VIII

Rob wàs standing on the gravel approach when she
arrived. He led her to the orchid house, opened the
door, and closed it with automatic care after they had
entered.

Then he checked himself with a grim little laugh.
'That's what's known as locking the stable door after
the orchid's bolted. Still, the tubers may as well be
protected even if the flowers have had it.'

She walked ahead of him to the spot where the cymbidium 'Doralinda' grew. At first she could see nothing
wrong, but as she came nearer she could see the colour
on one side of the flowers was quite different from the
other—darker and less pleasing. When she was close
to, the reason was quite clear: on the side of the petals
which had been towards the draught of frosty air from
the open door, the delicate fabric had become blotched
and darkened. On almost every bloom, one side of the
flower was wrecked by this change of colour and surface;
the two petals were spoiled, the sepals were withered
and crumpled, the lip of the orchid had lost its firmness.

'Oh, Rob!' was all she could say.

'A pretty complete write-off, eh? There may be six
blooms that aren't affected—but even those I wouldn't
like to guarantee, because the plants in this house simply
can't stand up to temperature changes like that.'

'How did it happen?'

He shook his head in perplexity. 'I simply can't
imagine. Everybody went home about midnight. I saw
them off, then went round making sure everything was in
order. I always do, before I go to bed.'

'And you noticed nothing?'

'Everything was absolutely normal.' He ran his hand
through his hair. 'This morning I got up about seven—
rather later than usual because I hadn't any orders from
any wholesalers or shops for today. I came out about

seven-thirty to turn on the sprinkler for the gladioli before the sun got round to them—and I noticed the door standing open.'

'Could it have . . . blown open?'

'Only if it wasn't properly latched—and when I tried it last night it was securely closed.'

'Did you hear anything after you went to bed?'

'No, but then I went straight to sleep. It had been a tiring day, one way and another.'

They stood silent, Lindy remembering the various emotional ordeals of Sunday and aware now that Rob too had had his trials.

'So someone could have walked in and opened the door,' she murmured at length.

'Easily. I never bother to close the gates at the entrance—why should I, when any determined intruder would only have to climb over? And I've never had locks put on the greenhouse doors because until now it's never been necessary. So anyone who wanted to create havoc among the orchids only had to stroll in, turn the handle, push the door wide, and walk away.'

'What time did you go to bed?'

'About one, I think.'

'So it must have happened later than that.' She was remembering that Lorenz had driven off in a rage soon after midnight: he could quite easily have gone back to Cramond. He would have arrived before one in the morning if he had gone straight there, but suppose he had driven around for a while, losing his way . . . or battling with his temper until finally he was pushed into vengeful action?

As she thought of this, she recoiled from it. She was unwilling to believe that Lorenz would do such a thing. But who else . . . ?

Marion, perhaps. Arnold had said he got home about one, a little earlier than he expected because someone else took Marion home. That meant she had no transport of her own.

'Rob, you were saying anyone " could have walked

in ". You mean you think the intruder came on foot?'

'Well, I feel sure I'd have heard a car drive in, no matter how soundly I was sleeping.' He considered for a moment. 'Naturally, the car might have been out on the road, waiting. I wouldn't hear a car draw up out there.'

Either way, Marion seemed to be ruled out. She had no car, and it was almost unbelievable that she could have walked the distance there and back in the middle of the night. From Cramond to Marion's home near The Meadows was at least five miles—ten miles, calculating the double journey.

Almost aimlessly Lindy moved along the greenhouse walk. Every plant seemed damaged—not only the orchid she had been planning to use but eight or ten others. 'Oh, how awful!' she whispered, looking at the wilted petals of white and orange and yellow and greenish-beige. 'It's like a massacre!'

Rob hunched his shoulders. 'I've got over it a bit. I felt a bit staggered when I first saw it.'

'Yes, it must have been—' She broke off, took his arm, pulled him close at her side. 'I'm so *sorry*, Rob. I think it's probably all my fault.'

'That's nonsense. How can you be blamed if some lunatic—'

'All the same, I do feel it's my fault. All these blooms—' She stopped short, struck by another thought. 'Rob, how much were they worth? The financial loss must be terrific.'

He glanced about. 'I hadn't got down to working that out. I suppose . . . at least four hundred pounds. Probably more.'

'Oh dear. Oh dear.' It seemed so inadequate. No words seemed to convey the stricken misery she felt.

'Don't take on so,' said Rob, putting his arm round her shoulders. 'A gardener is used to setbacks, you know. I remember once, when I was teaching in Cambridgeshire, a hailstorm knocked down the—'

'But that was an accident. This—*this* was deliberate.

141

To think of the time and money that's been reduced to nothing by it! Let's hope we can at least get back the money—you're insured, aren't you?'

'Yes, but—'

'But what?'

'If I make a claim, the insurance company will send a man to look at the damage—and he'll want to know how it happened and why I haven't called the police.'

'The police . . . ?' Naturally. He should have done so. This was a case of malicious damage. Why hadn't he called the police? She looked up into his face and she knew why: he thought Marion was responsible.

She was trying to think what to say about that—how to assure him it couldn't have been Marion without being too clumsy about the delicate and complicated relationships in the group, when he interrupted her train of thought.

In a determined, businesslike tone he said: "Putting all that aside, the problem remains—what are you going to use for the banquet?'

'Banquet?' she echoed; and then came to with a start. 'Oh, yes—tomorrow.' Incredible though it seemed, she had almost forgotten that she had to face this new hurdle. 'I don't know, Rob. I think . . . it'll have to be orchids. I can't start again from scratch with my design. I just . . . well, I haven't the time or the energy. Does that sound defeatist?'

'Not a bit. I understand just how you feel. Well, look, come to the other orchid house to see if anything would do as a stand-in.'

This greenhouse was much less warm than the one where the cymbidium had been growing; a glance at the thermometer showed her a temperature of sixty-five degrees, which was quite bearable even with the blue angora sweater she was wearing.

They walked slowly round the paved paths between the shelves. There were scores of plants in pots ranged like women in ball-gowns of a hundred hues; she paused as Rob gave her the names of those which were something like the colour of cymbidium ' Doralinda '. But always there was a drawback—either the blooms grew singly in an upright position quite unlike the falling, cascading trend she had envisaged, or if they were multiple blooms there were too few plants to achieve enough flowers for the massed effect she needed.

Finally Rob said: ' I can see I haven't got anything that will do. I'll tell you what—I can phone a few friends and see if—'

' No, no, there wouldn't be time. I'd have to go and look at them *today*, to be sure the flowers would do.' ' Besides,' she added inwardly, ' I want to use something of yours, to try to make up for what's happened.' But a second tour of the shelves left her with the same feeling: though there were many exotic blooms here, none of them had that simplicity and natural flow that she had seen in the dark red cymbidium.

As she was making her reluctant way towards the door a waft of pleasant, faintly almond-tinged scent made her pause. Glancing about to identify it, she discovered it was coming from overhead. From the ridge of the greenhouse three baskets hung down on short chains so that the plants were close to the light. Out of the basket cascaded the most remarkable blossom Lindy had ever seen—a pale yellow colour shading almost to cream, but looking like a cloud of cabbage-white butterflies hovering over a bush.

' What's that? ' she asked, pointing.

' Mm? ' He tilted his head. ' That's Stanhopea—called after Lord Stanhope, who was a medical botanist. Rather pretty effect, isn't it? Well, is there nothing here that will do for the banquet decor, Lindy? '

' Could I see those flowers at close quarters? ' she asked, gesturing at the hanging baskets.

' The Stanhopea? But, Lindy—' He broke off, shrugged, and went to a cleat on the side of the greenhouse where he undid a catch and lowered the basket of blossoms on its chain.

The flowers were really charming. The sepals were

143

folded back exactly like wings, and from the centre of this lovely upward-curving ring the lip of the blossom hung down, a strange clear white like the colour of sea-ice. There were about six blooms on each stem so that the effect, even close to, was of a group of butterflies.

'This one,' she breathed. 'I could use this one!'

'But my dear *girl*, you wanted something dark red—'

'Yes, but there isn't anything. I could use this—the ballroom has a lot of this ivory colour—' she touched the sepals—' and those little ringed spots on some of the petals give just a tinge of red.'

'I still don't see how you can make it work. White flowers on grey marble are going to look a bit funereal—'

'Red foliage. That's the answer. Red leaves. Something soft and *dull*—I mean with a dull surface.'

'Virginia creeper? But that doesn't hold its leaf when it's cut.'

'I could wire it. Who's got some Virginia creeper that's gone a good dark red?'

'I can easily get you some. There's a golf pro just down the road who has it growing all over his house. Mind you, it isn't *dark*.'

'No . . . I've got it! Copper beech!'

'That's easy. I've got a copper beech round the back of the house.' He stared at her. 'You really think it would look all right?'

'Yes,' she said, 'yes . . . Give me a stem of the flower, please, Rob.'

He picked up the secateurs, gently cut a spray.

'Now let's go and look at the beech tree.'

He led the way. The beech was growing at the far end of the garden, sheltering a few rows of vegetables. Once more he cut a spray and handed it to her. She borrowed the secateurs, snipped off a leaf here and there, then laid the flowers against the foliage.

'There!' she said in triumph.

The creamy-ivory flowers gleamed against the matt red of the leaves like pearls on velvet. She had a sudden sense of pleasure; this would be something remarkable

when she had finished the decor—soft, simple and yet
regal in its effect.

'Not bad,' Rob remarked, 'not bad at all. The beech
sprays are an awkward shape, though . . .'

'I'll trim them. Don't worry, it's not difficult to get
a shape with something as plentiful as beech leaves. It's
when you've got two stems of Eremusus that it gets
difficult!'

'Righto. Tomorrow morning, at the Darrin Hotel—
all the Stanhopea from the greenhouse and a stack of
copper beech.'

'That's it. We'll show 'em!'

Laughing, they made their way back to the drive
where her Mini was parked. After she had got in, he
handed her the spray of orchid he had cut. 'A consolation prize,' he said.

'Thank you.' With a wave she drove off, the white
Stanhopea lying on the passenger seat alongside, filling
the front of the Mini with its gentle, pervasive perfume.

When she got home she had only minutes to spare
before going out on one of her weekly assignments, the
flowers for the bank offices. But she spent those minutes
hastily sketching the outline of the new arrangement she
had envisaged—the beech leaves trimmed and curved so
that they would move in a sort of swirl, the orchids
poised among and over them as if in flight . . . Oh, it
would be so *pretty*!

As she went about the day's work she'd almost forgotten the reason for having to re-think her plans. The
new idea obsessed her; she pictured the way she would
place the outline branches, the fall of the blossom sprays.
Should she use some silvery leaves? One or two, perhaps—centaurea maritima—at least she could take some
with her tomorrow to see how it looked.

She ate lunch very late—getting on for three o'clock.
Mrs Ramsay, looking vexed, made her sit down to a
bowl of kidney soup and a salad with cold meat. 'And
here's the list of phone calls,' she said, putting the pad
down on the table some distance away, 'but mind and

no look at it till you've had your meal. I dinna want you leaping up to return a call while your soup gets cold.'

'All right, I'll be good, Mrs Ramsay.'

'Aye, likely! Well, I'm away now. See you to-morrow.'

The moment she had gone Lindy twitched the pad towards her, to glance down the list. Two names that meant nothing to her; then 'Mr Hemer 10.15' in that round, firm script; 'Mr Urquhart, to say thank you for today's flowers'; 'Mr H. again 12.10'; 'Miss Down-leigh re gift basket for hosp.—please ring' and the number; 'Mr H. *again*' heavily underlined; and lastly: 'A Mrs Aften-something, foreign—please ring.'

Lindy surveyed the catalogue. Well, she would *not* ring Lorenz. Presumably he was sorry for the quarrel yesterday and wanted to apologise. Did he also want to confess about the orchid-house and ask her forgiveness? If so, she didn't want to hear it. She was certain she couldn't speak to him about it without anger and a desire to punish.

She rang the numbers that were about business matters, accepted some orders, and went to her workroom to carry them out. Then she bathed and changed; she would deliver these flowers, then go straight on to hear Marion play at her first recital.

She chose a suit of soft dark blue wool with a matching ribbon plaited into her hair at the back. She hadn't decided what to do with the evening, so the outfit was suitable to go out to dinner, to go to a theatre or cinema, or simply to drive home and be comfortable by the television set. One thing was certain; she intended to be in bed by eleven o'clock. Tomorrow was a big day.

When she reached the venue for Marion's recital the audience—necessarily a small one—was almost complete. She saw Mrs Aftenwalden at the far side of the room, in the front row of chairs; beckoned by her, she threaded her way round.

'Ah, Lindy, where have you been all day? Lorenz is nearly beside himself.'

146

'Is he?' she replied unyieldingly.

The old woman fixed her with faded blue eyes. 'He thinks you told the maid to say you were out, because you didn't want to talk to him.'

'Is that why you rang? Did he ask you to?'

'Yes, he did, and that stupid woman at your house was most unhelpful.'

'She isn't stupid. She couldn't catch what you were saying.'

'So you were there all the time?' Mrs Aftenwalden accused.

'No, she told me when I got in, about three o'clock.'

'You got home at three? Then why did you not ring Lorenz?'

'Because I was very busy.' She felt like replying, 'Is it any business of yours?' but good manners to an older woman forbade it.

Mrs Aftenwalden wrinkled her nose in a charming, almost girlish grimace. 'I understand. A lovers' little tiff!'

'It was something more than that, Mrs Aftenwalden.'

'Ah? Serious?' She gave a little sideways motion of the head. 'Na, schön, you must make allowances. He says many things when he's in a temper that he regrets later.'

'We all do that. I quite understand that. But . . .'

'But what?'

She sighed. 'I'm not good at coping with it.'

'You will learn, my child, you will learn.'

'I don't think so. I find it so . . . degrading.'

'When he is angry?' Mrs Aftenwalden said in surprise.

'When he is jealous.'

'Ah.' There was a long pause. 'My dear,' she said, 'you must make up your mind to live with it. I am an old woman, I have seen many things, but I have never seen a man cured of a jealous nature.'

There was now a movement among the audience as the middle-aged man in charge of the arrangements glanced significantly at his watch, meaning that the recital was due to begin. Lindy nodded goodbye to Mrs Aftenwalden, then found herself a seat at the back. Across the foyer she saw the door slip open; Rob came in, to stand quietly beside it.

When Marion came in there was a spatter of applause. She was looking very pretty in a midi dress of olive green foulard, above which her silky-fine hair made a bright contrast. To Lindy's eye she seemed very tense. She bowed a little, sat down on the piano stool, made the little adjustments to the height that always seem necessary, then after clenching and unclenching her hands she began to play.

Lindy was no judge of piano technique and wasn't particularly keen on modern music, so she couldn't tell whether Marion was playing well or badly. She seemed to be more at ease in the second piece, a pastorale by a composer unromantically called Pinkham, according to the programme. She was raising her hands and her head at the end of an intricate passage when all at once her eye lighted on Lindy in the audience.

Her face changed. For a moment she seemed to hesitate, to forget where she was. Then automatically her fingers found the keys and after the minutest of hesitations the music flowed on.

But from that sudden startled, frightened expression, Lindy knew—it was Marion who had wrecked the orchids. The guilt had been plain to read on her face.

With sudden remembrance, Lindy looked across to Rob, to see if he had understood. But his angle of vision was not as clear as Lindy's; she was face-on to Marion, he was round somewhat to her right. He might not have seen that look, or understood it if he saw it. He was standing as before, leaning a little against a piece of panelled wall, head a little tilted, listening to the music.

The recital was to last forty-five minutes, with a five-minute break in the middle. At half-time, when the audience moved restlessly and coughed and consulted the programme, Lindy got up to make for the door.

'What's the matter, don't you like it?' Rob asked,

moving to meet her as she reached it.

'I'm not very musical.'

'Neither am I. I wonder if she's playing well?'

'No idea.'

'It seemed to me she lost her place somewhere in that second thing.'

'Did she? She made a quick recovery, then. Excuse me, Rob, I've got to go now.'

'Won't you stay and join the celebration afterwards? A group of us are going out to dinner in Frederick Street.'

'No, sorry, I've some business to attend to and then I want an early night.'

'Of course, for tomorrow's job. See you in the morning, then, at the hotel.'

She glanced over his shoulder as the room fell silent again, to see Marion come back to the instrument. She looked away quickly, for Marion's gaze was turned in their direction. With a whispered, 'So long,' she slipped out.

For her own satisfaction, she wanted to find out if she were right in her suspicions. She went home. Arnold was in the sitting-room, having a pre-dinner sherry. She shook her head as he got up to pour one for her and asked without preamble: 'Who was it who drove Marion home last night?'

'The Ormidales took her in their car—they live in that direction.'

'Thank you, Arnold.' She went out, carefully closing the door behind her. In the hall she looked up the Ormidales in the directory and rang their number. The phone was answered by Sophie, the girl whose field-glasses she had borrowed yesterday. After a few minutes' idle conversation—'Thanks for letting me borrow your binoculars', 'You were quite welcome', and so on—Lindy got to the point.

'You got home safely, did you?'

'Oh yes, quite. It was pretty late, though.'

'What about Marion? You gave her a lift?'

149

' Yes, but she asked to be put down at the Waverley. Said she wanted to look at the train arrivals board—at that time of night!'

' Goodness, what a funny thing. That must have delayed you.'

' No, she insisted we drove on—said she'd get a taxi home later.'

' At that hour of night?' Lindy said.

' Oh yes, there are one or two all-night cabs, you know—mostly for people who want to get to the airport for the night flights, I think.'

' I see. Oh well, nice talking to you, Sophie.'

When she had rung off, Lindy dialled the number of the information bureau. They furnished her with the name of the firm who ran an all-night service of taxis. She rang them, and when their booking clerk answered she took a deep breath and began to lie like a trooper.

' I wonder if you can help me? I took a taxi late last night from the Waverley, and I think I may have lost an earring in the car.'

' Oh yes, miss? Just a moment, I'll inquire.' A pause. ' Nothing's been found, miss.'

' Are you sure? I missed the ear-ring almost as soon as I got home.'

' Where was the journey to?'

' I went to Cramond, and then home to The Meadows.'

' Aye, I have that here—that was Tom McEvoy, he's not on duty yet. I'll ask him when he comes in.'

' No, please don't bother, they weren't expensive ear-rings and I can easily replace the lost one.'

' Are you sure now? Very well. Good evening, miss.'

So that was it! She had taken a taxi. As simple as that. Whipped on by an imperious need to punish Lindy for being luckier, a wish to make her life more difficult—and perhaps also to show her anger against Rob for daring to name the orchid after her—Marion had simply been driven back to Cramond, asked the driver to wait, carried out her stupid revenge and been driven home. Perhaps half an hour in all, on the empty late-night roads.

One thing Lindy was sure of: she must never tell Rob. He had said to her on a previous occasion: 'I think Marion is entitled to the benefit of the doubt' and though Lindy felt sure that this time he intuitively knew the culprit, yet to give him proof positive would be cruel. It would be hard to forgive someone who wrecked two years' work in one vengeful, thoughtless act.

Arnold appeared in the doorway of the sitting-room. He enquired: 'What are you looking so miserable about?'

'Nothing, Arnold, nothing.' She sighed. 'Have you ever heard those lines by William Blake?

'" Cruelty has a human heart,
And Jealousy a human face . . ." '

'I always thought those lines were about mercy and pity.'

'That was his first version, but he rewrote it. He'd learned, you see, by experience.'

'Dear me, you sound very disillusioned. You know, Lindy . . .'

'What?'

'It's astonishing how much more mature you've grown in the last few months.'

'Mature?' she said, summoning a smile. 'Like a matron?'

'Perhaps I should have said "less immature". You used always to seem rather . . . young for your age.'

'Which is why you wanted me married off to someone safe and reliable, like Rob.'

'I suppose so.' He tilted his head. 'There you are, you see? You can talk about Rob now without colouring up like a beetroot. That can't be bad, can it?'

'I suppose not.'

'What I came out to say was, if you've finished your phone calls, how about some dinner? Mrs Ramsay's left a casserole in the oven—I think she said it was venison, which is one of the joys of living here, isn't it? What other city can offer you venison on the daily menu?' Chattering with a rather forced brightness, which she knew was intended to cheer her up, he went into the kitchen.

The meal was served and cleared away by eight-thirty. Lindy was just consulting the television programmes when she heard the front door of the cottage open. It must be Rob: this was the way he usually appeared when he came calling.

She darted out of the sitting-room, exclaiming, 'Rob, has something happened—' but stopped short on coming face to face with Lorenz.

'You didn't ring me,' he said.

'No. I've been busy.'

'Too busy to get to a telephone?' His gaze rested on the instrument on the hall table.

She made no reply to that. 'Come into the sitting-room,' she invited, holding the door open.

He obeyed, but stopped short on seeing Arnold in one of the armchairs.

'Oh, hello, Lorenz,' Arnold said with cheerful indifference.

'Good evening.'

'We were just going to have coffee,' said Lindy, to cover the stiffness of his response. 'You'll have some, Lorenz?'

'Thank you.'

'I'll make it,' Arnold said. As he passed Lindy on his way out he raised his eyebrows expressively.

As soon as the door closed behind him Lorenz said: 'I must talk to you alone.'

'That's what you're doing now.'

'No, I mean properly—where we won't be interrupted.'

'That's rather difficult.'

'Come out with me. We can go for a walk—it's a lovely evening.'

'No, I'm sorry, I don't want to. Yesterday was rather

tiring and today has been no picnic. I just feel like an evening at home.'

'Lindy!' he said, his voice and features full of reproach.

'And I'll be tied up all day tomorrow and part of the evening, after which I think I'll be too tired to want to do anything but fall into bed.'

He studied her. 'You are punishing me,' he said.

'Perhaps I am. But mainly what I'm trying to do is show you that I have a busy and demanding life of my own, which I don't want made more complicated by continual quarrels and disagreements over nothing.'

'Is it nothing? When I see you looking with affection at another man?'

'You'll have to work that out for yourself, Lorenz. This I do know—one more outburst like yesterday, and I don't think I should want to see you again.'

'Lindy!'

'I'm sorry,' she said. 'Does it sound brutal? I can't help it. I never came up against jealousy until now, and I find I just can't bear it. It's too exhausting and destructive.'

'If you feel like that, think how I feel—'

'I've tried to. I've tried to understand what drives you to these flare-ups. But it's beyond me, I'm afraid. All I know is that I could easily stop loving you if it went on—because it makes you seem a stranger, and I can't love a stranger.'

'Then promise me—promise not to see Robert Blair any more, and I'll try to—'

'No. No promises, Lorenz. If I were to do that, I should end up never daring to speak to another man, or to be polite to someone introduced at a party.'

'But I should not be as foolish as that—'

'Wouldn't you? Can you guarantee that? Last night you were in a rage because I shook hands with Rob.'

'But that was different. You know he means something special to you. And he had just given you that new orchid.'

'Yes, he had. And unless you can accept things like that and live with them, it's no good.'

Arnold reappeared at that moment with the coffee-tray. He bustled about fetching the brandy from the sideboard to allow them a moment to recover; Lindy could see he guessed their conversation had been very serious. He looked questioningly at her, to learn whether she would like him to make himself scarce, but she gave a minute shake of the head. She didn't want a prolonged tête-à-tête with Lorenz; she had a feeling she might weaken, whereas there was safety in numbers.

She was determined to make a stand against Lorenz's emotional blackmail. She kept hearing the voice of Mrs Aftenwalden: 'I have never seen a man cured of a jealous nature . . .' If she gave in now she would never be able to make any headway against that possessive, exclusive love.

Lorenz accepted his coffee and a brandy. He made polite conversation until he had finished both, then took his leave. 'You are tired—I understand. It is better if I go.'

She made no demur. As she said goodnight to him he kissed first one hand, then the other. 'It will be different from now on. You shall see, *Hertzliebsten.*'

'I hope so, Lorenz. Good night.'

'*He* was very subdued, wasn't he—' Arnold remarked as she returned to her chair. 'It must have been a mother-and-father of a row you had!'

'How did you know we'd had a row?'

'Oh, my dear girl, one is not completely blind! He was spoiling for a fight all day yesterday. I kept wondering if he'd challenge Rob to a duel—it seemed the only outlet for all his fury and resentment.'

'Yesterday was a bad day . . . not only for me or for Lorenz.'

'Marion, you mean?'

She was startled. 'What about Marion?'

'You may well ask. Eventually she'll get over her

feeling that life has played her a dirty trick. She's got too much intelligence to go on forever being bitter. Having Rob to worry about her is a help, don't you agree?'

He talked on for a while about Marion and her problems. Lindy listened and nodded, but she didn't really want to discuss it. The problem of dealing with Lorenz had drained her emotional reserves. She was glad when she could with decency say that she must get to bed, and make her escape to her own room.

There, in a tall slender vase, she found the single spray of pale yellow Stanhopea that Rob had given her that morning. Strangely comforted by its presence, she went to sleep.

Next day the work at the Darrin Hotel was as demanding as she had foretold. Rob arrived at eight a.m. with the entire collection of *Stanhopea oculata* from his greenhouse; he had had the brilliant idea of simply detaching the three hanging baskets from their chains and attaching them to the inside roof of his van, so that they were still growing, fresh and vigorous, when they arrived. He had also brought vast quantities of copper beech, some Virginia creeper, some leaves of begonia rex, cyclamen silver-leaf, aralia elegantissima, and grevillea. She stared at the boxes laid open to view when he undid the back doors.

'Thought you might find some of it useful,' he said in a rather apologetic fashion. 'In case the beech leaves don't trim up just the way you want them.' He unloaded the boxes expertly, carrying them to the cloakroom she had been assigned as a workroom.

'The aralia is marvellous—the long thin leaves will counteract the beech's roundness. Thank you, Rob.'

'Okay, then, I'll clear off and leave you to it. If you need anything, give me a ring and I'll get it for you.' She took the last box and accompanied him to the door.

'Thank you, but I've got plenty of moss and wire and so forth. I think I'll be all right.'

She waved as he drove off, then went at once to work.

The first thing was the garlands for the front of the tables, which were to be set in a U-shape on three sides of the room only. She measured out the thick upholstery rope she had bought, marked and taped it at its fixing points, then laid it out on a trestle table. Next she had to clip and trim the beech twigs; all the pretty, delicate shapes she kept; all the short twigs and clippings were thrown into a tub of water to keep fresh, while she hammered and prepared the well-shaped pieces for the vases. She set these to have a long drink in deep old water jugs. Then, quickly and deftly, she took the reject-twigs one by one from the tub and wired them to the rope.

It was a long job, but by lunchtime she had a rope of dark red leaves, ready to have the flowers attached later.

At one o'clock Arnold arrived. 'Mrs Ramsay sent me to take you to lunch.'

She straightened, one hand in the small of her back. 'Mm? What time—? Oh yes. Lunch. Just let me wash up.'

Unexpectedly docile, she allowed herself to be taken to a meal in a Chinese restaurant. She didn't feel like talking, but did her best. She was glad to be allowed to get back to work.

In the afternoon she did the two vases for the two end tables of the U. They were quite tall and slim, in gold lustre and belonging to the hotel. She used some of Rob's begonia leaves to cover a frame of chicken wire and moss, and then from these evolved a Hogarth curve rising from each vase. They were no trouble; she turned next to low, tiny posies of apricot-coloured Brompton stock with two or three leaves of aralia, to be set at intervals down the length of the tables.

That left her free to work on the centre piece, the urn of Stanhopea which, set on its short column of polished grey marble, was to stand in front of the top table with the swags of leaves leading away from it. But she wanted to do that with the urn in position—to carry it after it was arranged and set it in its place would be impossible. It was now six o'clock. The hotel staff were finished with the cleaning and polishing, so now the tables could be laid with snowy-white damask and glittering silver.

She stood watching until it was done. Then she brought in the urn, set it up, packed in the moss, placed her first sprays of leaves, and thereafter was lost to the world as she worked.

She kept stepping back to view the effect, unaware that she was collecting an audience until she turned away to fetch the orchids. Then she discovered the head waiter, the receptionist, and Mr Urquhart were watching. She smiled at them absently, brought the orchids, and continued. A rising excitement gripped her; it was a magical arrangement, seeming to grow under her hands without effort.

When she had finished the shimmering, hovering cloud of orchids in its frame of red leaves, she paused. Now she must decide where to place the blossoms in the swag looped along the front of the tables. She brought in the rope of leaves, pinned it securely in its predetermined curves, and surveyed it. No problem—the places where the orchids must go in leapt to the eye. A few extra, feathery aralia leaves to soften the line here and there. A piece of sticky tape to hold a recalcitrant blossom. A spray of water to make sure the flowers wouldn't wilt when all the lights were on. And that was that. She whisked away the polythene that had been protecting the tablecloth.

Now that she had finished, she had no idea whether the effect was good or bad. To her it was too close, too much a part of her. But she could tell by the expression on George Urquhart's face that he was dazzled.

She wished all at once that Lorenz could be here, to see the work she had done and perhaps understand from that how important it was to her.

As if the wish had conjured him up, he came through the door of the ballroom.

' *Du lieber Gott!* ' he gasped. ' *Das ist aber wunder-*

schön!'

'You like it?'

'It is superb. I had no idea, Lindy, that you could do such a thing.'

'Oh, she has a great deal of talent, our Lindy,' said Rob, coming in at his elbow. He surveyed the decorations with pride. 'Not bad, not bad at all, considering this was only second-best!'

She laughed. 'Don't get carried away,' she said. She sighed and stretched. 'Lord, I'm tired!'

'No wonder. Come, we go to the hotel bar and you have a drink,' ordered Lorenz.

'No, no, please—the management would like to offer you a drink,' said Mr Urquhart. 'Please, I insist, Miss Gramont.'

He led the way into the stillroom, where a bottle of champagne was waiting in an ice bucket. He toasted Lindy and her flowers, Lindy toasted the success of the banquet; it was an occasion of great conviviality.

She was too tired to notice it at the time, but she remembered it as she fell into bed that night—Lorenz had behaved beautifully to Rob all through the little celebration.

Perhaps, after all, everything was going to be all right. Perhaps he'd got the better of his jealousy.

CHAPTER IX

All next day the phone was busy with messages of congratulation—from the photographer who took Mr Urquhart's publicity photos, from the wives of the Edinburgh businessmen who had attended the banquet, even from some of the businessmen themselves. There was no doubt that Lindy was thoroughly launched into a lucrative career in the city, if she should choose to stay here.

She was offered many immediate assignments, but chose not to take them. For the next few days she needed to rest: she had enough work in the regular commissions already booked, and it was time to relax a little, to catch up with the fun of the Festival.

So many attractions tempted her that she found it hard to choose. She went to the opera, to a late-night revue, to the Tattoo, a concert, an exhibition of avant-garde mobiles, a French farce, an after-the-show party at the Festival Club, an open-air dance, a midnight boating-party. She even showed a group of singers from the Kiev State Choir around Edinburgh Castle, reading bits out of the guide-book for the interpreter to translate.

Rob thought that event was hilarious. 'Talk about the halt leading the blind! What you don't know about Edinburgh Castle would fill an encyclopaedia!'

'I quite agree. I didn't ask to do it—you know the saying, "Some have greatness thrust upon them". It was very enjoyable, I must say. Castles intrigue me.' She glanced hopefully round the Sunday group at the Hundergate Hotel.

'Would you like to see another one?'

'Ye . . . es—where is it?'

'Here in Edinburgh. We're well off, you know—we've got several.'

'Have you?' She hesitated. 'Oh, you're pulling my leg.'

'No, no,' chorused the others. 'There's Craigmillar,

where Mary Stewart stayed. And Merchiston—'

'Oh, come on, that's only a ruin. There's enough without including heaps of stone,' said Rob. 'One afternoon when the weather's clear, I'll come and take you to see a castle, a special little castle that I know you'll enjoy.'

Lorenz said at once: 'Where is this place? I should like to take Lindy there.'

'Ah, no,' Rob replied teasingly, 'it's *my* castle. "I'm the king of the castle . . ."—'

'You own it?'

'No, no, Lorenz—it's a nursery game,' Lindy explained.

Lorenz looked vexed. 'These foolish little jokes . . .' he muttered, scarcely audible.

'No one could expect you to know things like that,' Marion put in, coming to his aid. 'I think you speak English marvellously well. I bet no one here could speak German up to the same standard.'

Rob laughed. 'All the German I know is concerned with climbing mountains,' he confessed. '*Alpenstock, Bergabhang*—things like that.'

'You have not climbed this summer, however,' said Lorenz.

'No. It's a bit difficult to get away at the height of the flower-growing season.'

'Perhaps you never really climbed very much.'

'Huh?' Rob looked surprised. 'Well, not much compared with the mad enthusiasts, I suppose.'

'Rob's darned good,' Hamish protested, darting an irritated glance at Lorenz. 'I've been on some terribly tricky rock-faces with him, and I can tell you—'

'Oh yes, he is of course very clever, we know that! He grows the most beautiful flowers in the world and he climbs the highest mountains in the world—'

'Lorenz,' Lindy said quickly, 'are you going to Lady Larchmound's musical party tomorrow?'

The difficult moment passed in general chat about the farewell party being given next day for the musicians of the Festival who had been able to stay an extra day or two. Yet all the same she could see that Lorenz was still prickly. She could understand to some extent—the Festival was over, for him there was a sense of let-down which made him ready to pick a quarrel.

After lunch they formed into groups and went off on their separate exploits. The weather was superb—an amber sunshine clothed the countryside.

'The view from the Castle would be gorgeous today,' Lindy said, recalling her tour of it with the Russian singers. 'The last time I was there, it was a bit cloudy, but even so it was—'

'Come then,' said Lorenz, 'I take you there.'

'We'll come too,' Marion added, taking Rob by his jacket sleeve and urging him towards his car.

'Oh, I don't know that I—'

'Rob would prefer only his special castle,' suggested Lorenz. 'Come, Lindy.'

With a shrug, Rob allowed himself to be included in the group headed for the Castle. They drove back to Edinburgh along roads carrying a fair amount of traffic as the Scots headed for the hills or the sea to enjoy the fine weather. The city itself was still busy; overseas tourists were still thronging Princes Street. They drove to the big car park in King's Stables Road, then went into the Gardens by a little gate giving access to a rough path at the very foot of the Castle rock.

Above them the rock towered. To their left, high above, were the parapets of the old fort, and on their left a ruin of the old Wellhouse Tower. Here the path became steep, curving and winding its way under the rock but up a slope which led eventually to the Castle Esplanade.

'Oh, look!' Lindy cried, her eye caught by a flutter of wings. 'Look, what's that on that branch?'

They all paused at a turn in the path, leaning against the handrail and glad of a chance to get their breath.

'A chaffinch,' Rob said. 'Look at it—having a real feast!'

In the thin soil that clothed the crag above them rowan trees, elder and ivy had taken root. On one of the trees a chaffinch was pulling at the expanse of re berries gleaming in the sun. As they watched, a pair of blue-tits settled on another branch and hung, upside down, pecking at the seeds.

'Who'd imagine you could come bird-watching a few hundred yards from Princes Street?' Lindy said in wonder.

'Oh, there are dozens of birds around here. Look up,' Rob said, pointing. 'See—in the actual walls of the fortifications?'

Now that her attention was drawn to them, she could see two or three pairs of pigeons roosting, their grey and-purple plumage merging perfectly into the brownish grey of the masonry.

'At night, you know, when the floodlights come on for the illuminations, you can see them rising in protest at being wakened up.'

'Really? How sweet! Do they get to sleep again?'

'Of course. There are lots of crannies in the stone work and in the rock itself, where they can get out of the beam of light.'

Lindy watched with intense pleasure as the small birds flitted in and out among the greenery above them. 'They know they're safe,' she remarked. 'No one but a mountain goat could ever get up there to disturb them.'

'I imagine there are all sorts of things growing in crevices on the Castlehill that no one's ever seen at close quarters,' Rob agreed.

'Yes, just look—there's a cluster of centaury growing up there.'

'Where?'

'To the right of the alder—a bit above it.'

'That pink thing?' Marion queried. 'That's ordin ary weed—that rosebay thing.'

'Well, I suppose centaury is a weed too, but I wouldn't expect to see it growing in the rock of Edin burgh Castle. In fact I don't think I've seen it at all since I came to Scotland.'

'Oh, it does grow in Scotland,' Rob told her, 'but usually on grassland. I think that flower up there is probably rosebay.'

'No, it isn't. Rosebay is more purple than that.'

'Climb up and find out,' Lorenz suggested in an ironic tone to Rob.

'Up there? You must be joking! It would be as slippery as a toboggan-run up there.' He linked arms with Marion. 'What's that German poem, Lorenz?— "Es stürzt der Fels . . ."'

'"The rock plunges",' Lorenz said, surprised. 'You know German poetry?'

'About ten lines. I'm better on English. How about "He clasps the crag with crooked hands"—only that's the eagle, not pigeons. They can all stay up there, birds and plants, as far as I'm concerned. Come on—onwards and upwards.'

They went on up the path, coming at last to a mere indentation in the grass running along below the scaffolding put up to hold the stands for the audience at the Tattoo. Workmen were already engaged in dismantling it. They went through the wicket gate on to the Esplanade, over the moat where two sentries of the K.O.S.B. stood on guard, past the statues of Robert Bruce and William Wallace, and into the Castle precincts, along by the battery of eighteenth-century cannon keeping ancient watch over the Low Defence.

Lindy had been right in prophesying a glorious view. Below them lay Princes Street and the straight, steep streets leading off to the north, towards the sparkling expanse of cold blue water where the River Forth flowed into the sea. Beyond that lay the hills of Fife, and beyond them still the hills of Perthshire.

'That's where we were, isn't it?' she asked, pointing north. 'Arnold's "dig"?'

'No, that's more to the west. I'm not quite sure, but if that very distant shape is Blairdenon, then we were a little west of that, on Dumyat, and the dig isn't far from there.'

'Dumyat—that was the place where you did a practice climb on that awful rock-tower—'

Lorenz made a sound of impatience. 'It was not anything so very awful. When you have two rock surfaces, a few feet apart, it is not difficult to go up—it is like climbing inside a chimney.'

Rob nodded and moved away. Lindy could see that he was anxious not to tangle with Lorenz. He stared out at the view, then brought his gaze back to the rock immediately below them.

'Look, there's the floodlighting I was telling you about —the lights that wake up the pigeons.'

'Where?' Marion asked, peering over at his elbow.

'On that parapet just below—I think those walls down there were called the "Close Fight", but now the only action they see is when the engineers fit up the lamps for the illuminations . . .'

'Then we must be above that piece of rock where the birds were having a feed on the rowanberries?'

'I think that's just below those old stone walls, a little to our left. Let's see . . . we're on Mill's Mount . . . Yes, that little patch of flowers and plants is down there.'

'From here it would be easy to go down and fetch the flower you pointed to,' Lorenz said to Lindy.

'Easy? No, it wouldn't!'

'But it would, my darling. Don't you see? One could go down a long way just by walking on top of those thick walls that go down the slope below us.'

She saw Rob shake his head as he overheard this. Lorenz caught the movement. 'You do not think it could be done?' he challenged.

'It could be done, but *I* shouldn't care to try it. It would be impossible to—'

'How can you say that? Impossible? It would be easy!'

And before anyone could stop him, Lorenz had swung himself over the parapet of Mill's Mount, dropped on to the broad surface of the wall of the Close Fight, and was running down it as if it was a garden path to the point where it ended, embedded in the rock itself.

Lindy watched, frozen in horror.

'Stop him!' screamed Marion. 'Lorenz, stop!'

Her cry jerked Lindy back to activity. She clutched Rob's arm. 'Rob, make him come back!'

He shook himself free. 'Why the devil should I? He's been spoiling for a chance to make a fool of himself for weeks. Well, now he's going to do it in the full glare of the public eye—and I hope he enjoys it.'

'But, Rob, he might be killed!'

He turned to stare at her. 'He's in no danger unless he jumps down from the wall—and even *he* has enough sense not to do that.'

She swung away from him. 'Lorenz! Lorenz! Come back!'

Lorenz, a lithe figure in slacks and blue sweater outlined against the backdrop of Princes Street and the Forth, waved an arm. 'I'm going to bring back your flower for you,' he called.

'No, no, I don't want it! Come on back, Lorenz!'

'Please come,' Marion shouted, cupping her hands like a speaking-trumpet. 'You might fall!' Her voice was harsh with strain and concern.

'Of course I will not fall! I'm going to climb down the wall to the rock-face—'

'Stop him, Rob,' Lindy pleaded. 'Tell him not to!'

'It's nothing to do with me,' Rob shrugged.

A figure in the uniform of custodian appeared at Lindy's side. 'What's all the noise about?' he inquired.

Rob waved a hand towards the figure on the parapet below. 'Some show-off, making an exhibition of himself,' he said in rather cruel amusement.

'Guid sakes!' The official, an elderly man, looked alarmed. 'Hi, you there! Come back! Come back this minute!'

'Easier said than done,' Rob remarked. 'You can shin down to the Close Fight, but you can't shin up again so easily.'

'I'll have to get the rescue team. Lord above, why *will* folk do things like this? Hi, you—stay where you are, I'll get a rope.' He hurried off, his square body moving with unexpected speed. Other visitors to the Castle drifted up, to stare in amazement and some admiration at Lorenz as he sat on the lower parapet, looking for a foothold in the stonework.'

'Lorenz!' Marion cried. 'Lorenz, don't do it!' She ran along to the angle of the walls, leaning over to see him clearly. 'You'll never get up again if you—'

'I shall be all right,' he replied, leaning back and waving. 'There are plenty of good cracks in the stone. See you in a minute.'

He turned, slid over the parapet, and hung by his hands. For a moment all that could be seen of him was head and shoulders as the overhang hid him. Then, as he had foretold, he found a crack in the wall for his foot. He went down a foot or two and came almost completely into view. He was about twelve or fourteen foot above the sloping basalt surface into which the wall had been built. His body edged its way down, towards the surface of tree tops which hid the rock.

Lindy glanced at Rob. She could tell from his calm regard that Lorenz was in no danger. She got back some of her own presence of mind so that when the custodian returned with another man carrying a rope she was able to reply with precision to their questions.

'He's climbing down the wall. There—see?'

'But where's he heading?'

'There's a clump of rowan trees and sycamore—below the floodlights, on the rock . . .'

'Oh, aye—*there*!' The two men looked at each other. 'It's going to take a commando to bring him back frae doon there!' They leaned over the wide parapet as far as they could, to track his descent.

Lorenz had reached the point where his searching foot had touched the rock. He gave a shout of triumph. 'I've made it!'

166

Lindy called back: 'Lorenz, don't go any further! Come back up the wall!'

'Nonsense! The clump of flowers is only a few yards away.'

For the first time Rob bestirred himself. 'Don't do it!' he shouted. 'That rock surface is covered in all sorts of grass and moss—you could easily slip!'

'He must be out of his mind,' muttered the official.

Lorenz's figure disappeared from view, masked by the contours of the rock and the leaves of the elder bushes. There was a tense silence, broken only by the distant sound of traffic in the town below.

'Lorenz!' Marion called in terror. 'Lorenz, where are you?'

His voice came from beneath them, muffled by the overhang. 'Here I am, safe and sound. I have your flower, Lindy.'

'What?'

'I have your flower—the little pink flower—*Ach, Himmel!*' There was a slithering, clattering sound.

'Lorenz! Lorenz, what's wrong?'

No reply.

'*Lorenz!*' It was Marion's voice, that last agonised cry. Lindy turned to push her way towards her at her vantage point on the wall's corner. But before she could reach her and offer comfort, Marion took matters into her own hands.

'Lorenz, are you hurt?' she called. 'Don't worry, darling—I'm coming!'

Next moment she had scrambled over the parapet and dropped to the Close Fight buttress ten feet below.

CHAPTER X

Lindy gave a cry of fear. For Lorenz she had been worried—for Marion she was terrified. She felt Rob brush past her, almost knocking her over by the speed of his movement. He took the rope from the castle official.

'I'll get her back,' he said.

'Hi, wait a minute, you'll only make things worse—'

'I'm a member of the Scottish Mountaineering Club.' Without waiting for more, Rob swung himself over the wall, the rope linked over his arm.

Lindy watched with fascinated horror. Marion, having reached the broad surface of the Close Fight buttress, was crouched now in frightened immobility, panic-stricken by finding herself outside the safe confines of the Castle's steep buildings. Rob landed beside her. She looked up, startled. He undid the rope, passed a loop round her, fastened it securely, then threw the main coil up to the helpers on Mills Mount.

'Up you go,' Lindy heard him say cheerfully. 'You'll be all right—don't worry. Put your feet against the surface of the stones . . . That's right. Use your hands to keep yourself from knocking against the wall as they pull you up . . . And don't look down. Ready?'

Marion's reply was inaudible.

'Okay,' Rob called. 'Haul away—*slowly*, mind.'

Soldiers from the barracks had joined the small crowd around Lindy. They took the rope and pulled, to the instructions of a sergeant. In about ninety seconds Marion was being helped back to the safety of the gun terrace on Mills Mount. She was trembling, white and stiff-faced with reaction.

'It's awful down there,' she whispered, 'it's awful—there's miles and miles of space below you . . .'

'Come along, miss,' said the custodian. 'You come into the first aid room—we'll get you a nice cup of tea.'

He led her away.

The sergeant leaned over. 'Hi, below? Are you coming up?'

Rob shook his head. 'I'll go and see what's happened to my friend.'

'Oh, aye, he's a friend o' yours? D'you want the rope?'

'Not at the moment. I'll go down to the end of the wall and see what I can see. I'll be back in a minute.'

He walked along the sloping surface of the battlement until he came to the point where Lorenz had climbed down. Here he squatted, peering into the undergrowth below.

'Lorenz? You okay?' he called.

Lindy could hear no reply, but it was clear Lorenz had answered, for Rob carried on a conversation that was only partly audible. After about five minutes he came back to the point just below the wall of the Mills Mount gun emplacement.

'He slipped and he's gone down about twenty feet,' he reported. 'I can't see him, but I can hear him. He says he's hanging on to a tree root or something.'

'Is he hurt, then?' inquired the sergeant.

'Only scratched and bruised, I think. He sounds fit enough to me.' Rob's voice was hard. 'I'd say he's getting tired, though—hanging on to a tree that's only anchored in a few inches of soil over rock is a nerve-racking business.'

'Oh, Rob,' Lindy burst out in alarm. 'Will the tree hold?'

'We'll have to hope so. It's probably that little rowan where we saw the chaffinches, or maybe one of those young sycamores.'

'How are we going to get him up?' the sergeant inquired.

'Oh, he can't come up. He'll have to go down—we'll have to lower him to the path below.'

'We'd better inform the police,' said the man who had come with the rope. 'If anything goes wrong . . .'

'We haven't got time to wait for the police,' said Rob. 'If that tree pulls loose, he'll fall fifty feet.'

'Heh!' said the sergeant expressively. 'We'd better get a move on. You seem to know a bit about climbing —what should we do?'

'We'll need another rope. This one's too short. I'll take this one and go down to him. You lower another one—and make it a good long one, to take us down to the path.'

'But if you reach him, sir, surely the wee tree will be too weak to hold the both of you?'

'Don't worry. I'll be tied to something substantial. *I've* no desire to fall down and break my crown.'

He coiled up the rope and went back over the parapet. With neat, quick steps he made his way along the battlement below. He clambered down into the area within the battlement where the floodlights were standing. After testing one or two pieces of equipment, he stopped by an iron stanchion; Lindy saw him tie one end of the rope to that. Then he went nimbly up the wall and down the other side, and in a moment was lost to sight as he went among the greenery on the rock.

The soldiers had split themselves into two groups— one had gone to fetch some equipment, the others were shepherding the bystanders away from the area of activity.

'You'd better go, miss. You're only in the way here,' the sergeant said, not unkindly.

She nodded mute assent and walked off, surprised to find she could move at all. Once on her way, she was seized with an idiotic sense of urgency—a feeling that if she didn't act with speed and decision, everything would go wrong. She began to run without quite knowing where she was running to—and five minutes later found herself at that elbow bend in the path below Mills Mount, from which they had watched the birds feeding on the berries.

Gasping for breath, she set her back against the wooden handrail and looked up. Grasses, old-man'sbeard, the rustling leaves of the sycamore, a mossy angle of rock, ivy and ash-tree . . . Where was Lorenz? Where was Rob?

Then she saw the pigeons wheeling in protest, and caught a glimpse of Lorenz's sky-blue sweater.

She wanted to call out, to ask if everything was all right. But her throat was parched with fear, she was too breathless after her run. She leaned back and stared upwards.

A few minutes later two police constables came hurrying along the path. They followed her gaze.

'Can you see them?' one asked.

'The patch of blue——'

'Oh aye, I've got them. Anything happening?'

'Not so far.'

Two ordinary passers-by, coming uphill from the Gardens, paused to stare at whatever the policemen were staring at. As if by magic a small crowd of about ten people collected.

Lindy was quite unconscious of their presence. She strained to watch the scrap of blue which she knew was Lorenz's sweater. It seemed to her that hours passed before it began to inch downwards. Almost at once it disappeared from view, hidden by the bushes. Then there was a patch of bare volcanic rock, and as he crossed that Lorenz was plain to see—scratched, dishevelled, his clothes stained with moss and earth, but safe and sound.

He came down gingerly, the rope extended only a little at a time and sometimes tangling in brushwood or catching on a rock. But after what seemed like a century, he reached the little expanse of grass at the foot of the drop. The two policemen guided him to a standstill, untied the rope.

'You all right?'

'Thank you, yes.' He turned to Lindy. 'Were you worried about me, *Liebchen*?'

'Oh, *Lorenz* . . .'

The constables were holding the rope taut and looking

up. Although Lorenz was saying something, she paid no attention—she was watching for Rob to appear.

He came down the steep rocky incline in what seemed seconds, using the rope like a kind of balustrade. The two policemen, who had been going to help him as they had helped Lorenz, stood back. He reached the grass, gave three jerks on the rope, and it slowly dragged itself up out of sight. Then he turned to join the group on the path.

'I have to admit that you were right,' Lorenz said on a note of apologetic amusement. 'And I must thank you—'

'I don't want your thanks,' said Rob. His face was dark with anger. 'It's no pleasure to me to be proved right in a thing like this. It seems to me, Hemer, that you're the most conceited, self-centred idiot I've ever met, and next time you get stuck in a jam like this I'll take care not to be around to rescue you.'

'Rob!' exclaimed Lindy, aghast. 'You can't—'

'Oh, can't I? Lorenz isn't the only person who can throw a temperament! I've been waiting to tell him what I thought of him for weeks now—and while I'm about it I may as well finish the job. Any woman who can get in a state over a man like that must be as silly and shallow as he is, so you're a well-matched pair. I wish you joy of each other!'

He wheeled and walked away. Bereft of speech, Lindy watched him go. Never in her life had she imagined that Robert Blair could behave like that. She simply couldn't believe that it had happened. She stood in a daze, wondering if it was all a nightmare from which she would waken by and by, only to be roused by a question from one of the policemen.

'What? Yes, of course I know who he was,' she said. 'His name is . . . is . . .' But she found to her dismay that she couldn't finish. Unexpected and overwhelming, tears poured from her eyes and choked her voice. She covered her face with her hands, leaning blindly against the broad blue-clad chest of the constable.

'There, there,' he said in consternation, 'dinna greet. It's a' finished. Come on, Tam, we'll take her home—she's upset, poor wee thing.'

Yes, indeed she was upset. Arnold couldn't make head nor tail of her state of mind when he at last got her to tell him what had happened.

'So nobody was hurt?'

'No.'

'So there's nothing to be distressed about.'

'I'm not distressed.'

'Then why are your eyes so red? Why haven't you eaten any dinner?'

'I don't feel like eating.'

'Look, I quite understand that it frightened you to see Lorenz in danger, but it's all over now. Do be reasonable, Lindy.'

'I don't feel like being reasonable.'

'Then what do you feel like?' demanded her brother in exasperation.

'I feel like being left alone. Is that too much to ask?'

'All right, all right, don't be tetchy about it. One is only trying to be helpful—'

'Helpful? Do you call it helpful to go prattling on and on—'

'Dear me,

"I am ashamed that women are so simple
To offer war where they should kneel for peace",

as the Bard says.'

'I'm sorry, Arnold,' she said, contrite. 'I really don't know what's the matter with me.'

'It's shock, no doubt. I daresay it would be better for you not to have to talk. I'll go out, shall I, and leave you in peace?'

'I don't want to drive you out of your own home . . .'

'Nonsense, nonsense. In any case, one would like to know how Marion is feeling after all this turmoil. So long, my pet. Find yourself a nice book and go to bed with a hot drink—it's probably what you need.'

This advice seemed sound, and she therefore endeavoured to take it. She found a copy of *The Mill on the Floss* in the bookcase, took it up to her bedroom, turned down the bed, and switched on the bedside lamp. Then she went to the kitchen to heat some milk. Meg Merrilies, the little cat, rubbed against her ankles as she stood by the stove keeping watch on the saucepan.

'You love me, Meg, don't you?' she asked, reaching down to pet her.

Meg purred ecstatically.

'That's right. Even if Rob Blair thinks I'm silly and my brother thinks I'm tetchy . . .'

She tried to examine her own feelings. She seemed to be in a great emotional muddle, but exactly why, she couldn't explain. When Lorenz had climbed over that parapet this afternoon she had been alarmed, really shaken; and when Marion so foolishly went after him she had been so frightened and anxious that she hadn't known what to do.

But the extraordinary thing was that she had been *more* worried about Marion than about Lorenz. She had been afraid Lorenz might get hurt, of course; and she had been relieved when he was brought down to earth safe and sound. But there hadn't been the same knife-thrust of fear for him as she had felt for Marion.

That was because Marion was totally inexperienced in climbing. There had been more reason to be afraid for her than for Lorenz.

But did reason have much to do with the feelings of people in love?

The boiling milk rose in the saucepan to cascade, unchecked, over the sides. Exclaiming in annoyance, she snatched the pan off the range. Really, why was she day-dreaming like this? Couldn't she even do a simple thing like prepare a bedtime drink?

She poured the milk into a mug, then ran water into the saucepan. Just as she was about to go upstairs with the drink she heard the front door open.

Arnold was back very soon, surely? 'Is that you,

Arnold?'

'No, it's me.' The kitchen door opened and Lorenz came in.

She experienced a sinking of spirits. She simply didn't feel up to coping with Lorenz tonight.

Nevertheless, she summoned a smile. 'I was just going to bed,' she said, holding up the steaming mug of milk.

'So early? It's only a little after nine.'

'Arnold thought it would do me good to have an early night.'

'Ha, of course, you have been very upset. It was a wearing experience, wasn't it?'

She shrugged. 'What did the police say?'

'Oh, they took me aside and asked my name and address and said I might be hearing from them. It seems I committed some sort of offence, by climbing the Castle walls.'

'Did you? Trespass, perhaps. Or damage to Crown property.'

'I don't really think anything will come of it. I hope not. I made a big enough fool of myself without having to appear in court and pay a fine.'

She didn't know whether to agree with him or not, so she said nothing.

He went on: 'At least one good thing has come of it.'

'Oh?'

'Oh yes. Now I am sure you love me.'

She gazed at him, her brow wrinkled in perplexity. 'What happened to make you say that?'

'You would not have been in tears afterwards if you had not been very tense and anxious about me. That is quite clear.'

'No, Lorenz, I don't think you can—'

'Ah, my darling,' he said. He stepped close to her, took the beaker of milk and put it on the kitchen table. He had only to take one step closer to be able to kiss her.

At that moment Meg Merrilies decided to thrust herself between them in hopes of being stroked again by Lindy. Startled, Lorenz looked down, moved sharply. The cat wove round his foot so that he stumbled.

He kicked at her. '*Törichte Tier!*' he exclaimed.

Meg ran away, miaowing in alarm.

'Don't do that!' Lindy cried. 'She didn't mean any harm.'

'She nearly tripped me up—'

'Here, puss, puss, puss—'

'Oh, stop calling to that stupid animal and listen to what I'm saying—'

'She isn't a stupid animal. And I don't *want* to listen to you.'

'Lindy!' he gasped.

She had been stooping to talk to the cat. Now she straightened, looking him straight in the face.

'I mean it. I don't want to listen to you, Lorenz. I've had enough for one day. I'd like you to go.'

'But—but—you don't know what it was I came to say.'

'I got the gist. You're sure now that I love you because I burst into tears this afternoon.'

'Yes, and so I have decided that we are really meant for each other and we must get married.'

'Really?'

'Yes,' he said, missing the dryness in her tone. 'I have the chance of a new post, a very good one, in Salzburg. We will be married before I go there.'

'I don't think so, Lorenz.'

'*Wie?* What did you say?'

She moved her head from side to side, so that her long chestnut hair swung against her neck. 'I don't want to marry you.'

'But—'

'A couple of months ago, if you'd asked me, I would have been so happy. When you asked me to go to London—remember?'

'Yes, but then I was not sure . . .'

'That you wanted marriage?'

He coloured. 'A man does not think of marriage as quickly as a woman does, Lindy. I admit I was wrong. It was only when I realised I might lose you to Robert Blair that I began to think I could blend my life with yours. But even so, I wanted to be sure you really loved me.'

'So now that I've passed all the tests, you're proposing to me.'

'Yes, proposing—that is the word. Now don't be mischievous, Lindy. Don't tease me any more by refusing.'

'I'm not teasing you, Lorenz, believe me.' She sighed. 'Perhaps if you'd asked me even yesterday, I'd have said yes. But today the answer is no. Absolutely and definitely, no.'

'But—but why? *Why?* You love me, Lindy!'

She gave a wry little smile. 'I'm afraid not. I'm not even sure that I like you.'

'Lindy!'

'You remember I told you I found it difficult to be fond of someone who was continually jealous.'

'Yes, but now that I am sure you love me—'

'It's all different, is it? Until the next time something makes you uncertain. How often would I have to prove my feelings to you?'

'Oh, but, my darling, there would be no more problems—'

'I think there would. I'm not at all sure that you and I could make each other happy. I can't feel kindly towards a man who's always causing scenes, who gets into childish tantrums—'

'Lindy, that is enough! You dare to call me childish?'

'That was pretty childish this afternoon, wasn't it?'

'That only happened because I was angry—'

'It happened because you wanted to show off. And because of that you endangered other people's lives.'

'Oh, now we are back at Rob again!'

'Rob was never in any danger—he knew what he was doing from the moment he went over that parapet. It was Marion I was thinking of.'

'Marion?'

'You don't even know that she went rushing after you? She was in a terrible state.'

'My dear girl, if Marion chooses to behave foolishly it's nothing to do with me.'

'Of course it's to do with you! It's because she's still head over heels in love with you, despite the fact that you dropped her so callously.'

'Oh, so now you are going to blame me because I cannot love Marion?'

'No, Lorenz,' she said in a weary voice, 'I'm not blaming you for not loving Marion, any more than I'm blaming myself for not loving you. It's just one of those things that happen—we think we feel a particular emotion, but either we change or the emotion does. All I know is that I don't love you. I can't explain it or account for it. I think I've been growing out of love with you for quite a while, but today was the end.'

'Because I wanted to climb down the rock to bring you a flower?' he asked, with the coaxing of a small boy in his manner.

'Because . . . because you kicked Meg Merrilies. Because you shrugged off Marion and her heartache. Oh, I don't know. Whatever the reason, it's finished, Lorenz.'

'Not for me,' he insisted. 'Not for me.'

'I'm sorry. As you said about Marion—it's nothing to do with me.'

The bright, penetrating gaze of his grey-green eyes dwelt lingeringly upon her. His expression was bewildered, hurt. 'You *have* changed,' he said, 'I did not know you could be so hard. The girl I fell in love with was more gentle, more . . .'

'Immature? My brother told me I'd grown up a lot recently. Perhaps it was time I did. Goodbye, Lorenz.'

'Oh, no, Lindy, we can't part like this—'

'It's best. Honestly, there's nothing more to be said. I'm sorry if you think I'm hard, but it would only be cowardice if I shirked this issue—and I'm finished with being a coward.'

She opened the door of the kitchen, went into the hall; he followed. 'Goodbye, Lorenz,' she repeated.

He made no reply. He stood for a long moment as if waiting for her to recall the word. When she did not, he grasped her in his arms like hoops of steel and kissed her fiercely, intensely.

She suffered it to happen. She stood in his embrace, wooden and unresponsive.

When he let her go, she said: 'Goodbye, Lorenz.'

Emotions fought for supremacy in his face: astonishment, distress, anger, indignation. She was afraid of some furious outburst, but stood firm.

His eyes narrowed. He shrugged, then he walked out of the house without speaking.

She went upstairs a few minutes later, washed, and got into bed. Though she opened the book, and stared at page one, she read never a word. At last, when she heard Arnold come in, she put out her light and pretended to be asleep because she didn't want to have to talk to him. But it was a long time before sleep came.

But she slept late next morning. Arnold had gone out by the time she came downstairs. Mrs Ramsay was polishing the brass letterbox and bell-pull on the front door, singing 'The Bonnie Wells o' Wearie' in a loud, cheerful voice. The cat was sitting, as the schoolbooks say, on the mat, allowing the morning air to ruffle her tabby coat.

''Morning, Meggie,' said Lindy, bending over her. 'Quite recovered from being kicked?'

Mrs Ramsay turned. 'Wha kicked her?' Her face went an indignant pink. 'Och, ye needna tell me. It was your Mr Hemer.'

Lindy was surprised. 'What makes you say that?'

'Wha else that comes here would kick her? It's no my business, Miss Gramont, but I'm telling you all the

same—yon fellow's just like a spoilt child, and if he'd
'a' been mine, I'd have gie'd him a skelpit leathering.'

'A what?'

'A . . . a . . .' The other woman hesitated, brushed
back a strand of hair with her forearm, then gave a
giggle. 'It means a spanking. I shouldn't have said
that, it's disrespectful. I apologise, Miss Gramont.'

'It's all right, Mrs Ramsay. I quite agree Mr Hemer
was probably spoilt as a child.'

'Ye do?' A pause. 'Eh . . . well then . . . is he
still your fellow?'

Lindy sighed. 'No, Mrs Ramsay, he is not.'

'An' you're no heartbroken?'

'It seems not.'

'Well, isn't that grand? I'm that pleased to hear it!
Atween you and me,' Mrs Ramsay said confidentially, 'I
never liked him. Meg Merrilies never took to him, ye
ken—she never let him stroke her. They're very sensitive, cats are!'

Lindy was divided between laughter and regret. It
seemed absurd that she had wasted so much time and
heartache on a man that the little cat had refused to
approve of.

'Is it your breakfast you're wanting now? I'll just
put away the metal polish and wash my hands.' Mrs
Ramsay bustled into the kitchen, poked at the fire in the
steel range. 'Tea or coffee?'

'Tea, please. Mrs Ramsay, aren't you surprised that
I shan't be seeing Mr Hemer any more?'

'Gracious, no. He made you all up-and-down in your
feelings—one day in heaven, the next day the other
place.' She gestured downwards. 'Yon's no way to
live your life. Na, na,' she said, picking up the steaming kettle, 'you've too much gentleness in ye to cope
with a man like Mr Hemer—he'd scar you for ever. You
need someone who thinks less of himself and more of
you.'

'I don't know,' Lindy sighed. 'I just seem to keep
making a mess of my romances.'

'Is that a fact? How many have you had?'

'Well . . . two.'

'Third time lucky, mebbe.' Mrs Ramsay seemed to
stop for a moment in thought, then said with determination, 'It's a man like Mr Blair you should marry.'

Lindy shook her head. 'That's not likely.'

'What for no?'

'He's got a low opinion of me.'

Mrs Ramsay gave a snort of derision. 'Never heard
such nonsense. He worships the ground you walk on.'

'Oh no.' Lindy coloured. 'Yesterday he said—'

'What he *says* and what he *feels* are twa fine things,'
said the older woman firmly. 'I'd have thought you'd
know that yourself—you dinna always say exactly what
you feel, do you?'

Lindy made no reply. Mrs Ramsay poured her tea,
set it before her, went to the door, and hovered. 'I'm
going to dust the sitting-room . . . Think well on what I
said, Miss Gramont.'

Think about it? It was impossible to get it out of her
mind all morning. In the end, to distract herself, she
went out to call on Marion; she owed her at least the
courtesy of a visit to see how she felt after yesterday's
adventure.

She walked to the crescent on the other side of town
where Marion lived. The day was cool, with a strong
west wind blowing. She wrapped herself deeper into
her coat of toast-coloured tweed and felt noble at taking
all this trouble to visit a girl she didn't even like.

Marion herself opened the door to her. She was surprised to see her visitor, and not particularly pleased.

'I just thought I'd drop in to ask how you were.'

'Thank you, it's very kind. I'm all right.' She
hesitated. 'Do you want to come in?'

'Please.'

Rather ungraciously Marion led the way to a vast,
high-ceilinged sitting-room dominated by a grand piano
at one end. 'I was working,' she said. 'Please sit
down. Can I get you some coffee?'

'No, thanks, I've only just had breakfast. Wha
happened yesterday? I went—'

'You went rushing off to be with Lorenz.'

'No,' Lindy said, her voice shaking as she looked
back on the events of yesterday. 'That wasn't why
rushed away.'

She knew, now that she was brought face to face with
the memory, that she had been panic-stricken until she
saw Rob come safely down from the Castle rock—just
as she had been panic-stricken when she thought he was
in danger on the short rock-face on Dumyat. It had
been Rob she was really worried about. It had been
Rob's words that hurt her.

'What's the matter?' Marion inquired. 'You look
quite upset.' Her manner softened a little. 'I suppose
yesterday was a bit of an ordeal for you too.'

'Yesterday was a dreadful day. I . . . I broke it off
with Lorenz, finally and for ever.'

'What?' The other girl leapt up, knocking music
manuscripts to the floor. 'You did what?'

'He came to see me and . . . and . . . it just all came
to an end for me.'

Marion went to the window. She stood for a while
with her back to Lindy. 'Did you come on purpose to
tell me this?'

'No. I came . . . in a way I came because I feel I
owe it to you. Without intending to, I've done you a lot
of harm, Marion. I'm truly sorry.'

'Sorry?' The voice was bitter. 'Do you think that
cancels it all out?'

'I never meant you to be unhappy. I didn't know
at first that you and Lorenz—'

'And now you think, because you don't want him
that it's all right for me to have him back?' She swung
back to stare at Lindy. 'It's not as easy as that. Yes
terday made me think a lot. I was so *frightened* when
I found myself out on that escarpment . . .'

'It was a mad thing to do, Marion.'

'One of many. And all because of Lorenz.' She

opped short, in doubt what to say.

Lindy came to her aid. 'I know it was you who recked the orchids.'

'You—? But how could you know?' The little iangular face flamed with humiliation. 'And Rob? oes he know?'

'I think he guessed.'

'I must have been out of my mind. It cost him so uch, in time and money wasted. And he's been so ood to me.' Marion put up her hands to cover her face. 'I'm so ashamed.'

'Don't, my dear.' Lindy got up and came to her. Don't make yourself unhappy about it.' She put her m round the slim shoulders.

'It's just that it all seems so futile,' Marion whispered. Lorenz isn't ever going to love me. I see that now.'

'I'm afraid that's true, Marion.'

'He didn't even bother to ring and find out how I as after yesterday. Rob rang, and Arnold came last ght—but Lorenz didn't bother.'

'If you could just accept the fact that he's by no eans as wonderful as you imagine . . .'

'That's easy for you. You've got so much else in ur life—your career, your nice brother, and Rob . . .'

'Rob?'

'Of course. Rob thinks about you all the time.'

'Oh, no, I don't believe . . .'

'Why else do you think I got so jealous and angry? thought I'd found someone who would make up to me r losing Lorenz, but all the time I knew in my heart at Rob was only being kind to me, that it was you he red about.'

Lindy felt once again that wave of emotion—half iumph, half uncertainty—that had washed over her hen Mrs Ramsay said almost the same thing. Unable speak about it, she led Marion to the sofa. They sat wn, and she began to coax information about Marion's ans for the future. She intended to teach music, per- aps privately; she might even turn to composing by and by.

They parted half an hour later, better friends tha
they had ever been before. Lindy was pleased that sh
had made the effort to get to know her; the awful sens
of guilt on Marion's behalf was gone at last.

That evening was Lady Larchmound's party. Lind
had an invitation, but was in two minds whether to go—
because Lorenz would be there. In the end she decide
that if she didn't go it would be like running away, s
she put on a new dress of silver jersey, piled her hai
into a silver net, touched her nails with silvery polis
and—feeling as if she were wearing silver armour—wer
to Lady Larchmound's with Arnold.

The place was over-full. The room was hot an
smoky. Everyone was talking too loud, and mostly i
foreign languages. She needn't have worried abou
meeting Lorenz, because he didn't come; instead sh
found herself cornered by Mrs Aftenwalden who said i
a whisper she could scarcely catch, 'You have heard th
news?'

'What news?'

'About Lorenz.'

'No, what?'

'He hasn't told you? He rang me . . .' The rest wa
lost in the surrounding babble.

Finally Lindy managed to bring her head almost on
level with the old lady's lips. What she was telling her
she insisted, was strictly in confidence—but Lorenz ha
accepted the job.

'What job?' Her mind made a leap. 'In Salzburg?

Mrs Aftenwalden nodded impressively. 'Shall yo
like living there?' she inquired.

Lindy sighed, and considered explaining that sh
wouldn't be going, but in the circumstances decided i
would be difficult. So she shook her head and shrugged
then made her escape.

At the far side of the room she could see Mario
McColl in conversation with her brother. She wondere
if Marion had heard the news. Really it was best fo

everyone that Lorenz should go, but most of all for Marion who might, once he was removed from her circle of friends, eventually get over him.

As September progressed, it became important to Lindy to make up her mind what she intended to do with her career. Christmas was on the way; already she was being asked to do flowers for balls and parties, for New Year celebrations. If she wanted them, she had assignments to take her on into February and March of next year.

Did she want to stay in Edinburgh?

Well, why not? She had made many friends. She could have a fine career. She liked the city, the surroundings, the social life. Once Lorenz had gone—and she heard on the grapevine that he was leaving in October—there would be nothing to prevent her having a very enjoyable life here.

But she knew very well why she was hesitating. She needed to know where she stood with Rob. Since that painful moment after the escapade on the Castle rock, he had been avoiding her. They had seen each other, but only when the usual crowd was around. He had scarcely spoken a word to her even then. She couldn't tell whether he was still angry, or embarrassed, or what—all she knew was that if anything was to happen between them, she would have to make the first move.

One Sunday they had all gathered for lunch at the Hundergate Hotel. It was a day of sharp autumn weather, still and fine but with a nip in the air. The golfers on Gullane's links were zipped into their windcheaters and wore gloves—'a sure sign of winter when the golfers start to wear gloves,' Hamish said.

'What are we doing this afternoon?' said Arnold. 'If any of you have time to spare perhaps you'd come home with me and help with the cataloguing. I'll be closing the dig next weekend.'

One or two enthusiasts volunteered to do a page or two of the catalogue. To Lindy's surprise, Marion was among them.

' How about you, Rob?' Lindy asked.

Rob shook his head.

Lindy gathered her courage. ' Remember you once offered to show me a castle?' she said.

He met her eyes. ' Yes?'

' Can we go today?'

He studied her. He gave a little half-smile. ' Today's a good day. Most of the tourists have gone—we'll have the place to ourselves. It's at its best when there's no one there.'

' It sounds intriguing. I'd love to come.'

He looked suddenly doubtful. ' I hope you'll like it,' he said.

When the meal was over they sorted themselves out, as usual, into varying groups. Rob said little until they had come to the outskirts of the city. Then he inquired, ' How's the work going?'

' Plenty of it. How about you?'

' Same here. Thanks to those publicity photos of Urquhart's I've had a spate of orders for the orchids.'

' That's good.'

' Well, yes, it is. It means the business is really going to do well. It's been a bit of a gamble, you know, specialising in rare blossoms—they're expensive to raise and difficult to market. But this year, one way and another, I've been able to do more than break even.' He paused. ' A lot of it is thanks to you, Lindy.'

' Me?' she echoed, surprised.

' Your work has brought rare flowers into demand. People have been able to see, perhaps for the first time, that it's worth paying for the blossoms because the result is a real work of art.'

' Oh . . . Thank you.' She was blushing with pleasure and embarrassment. To ease the situation she said suddenly, ' We're heading towards Cramond—are we going to your place?'

' Not quite. You'll see in a minute.'

They came into Cramond Road South from Barnton Park, and almost at once he slowed and signalled a right turn. There were big gateposts and a sign saying 'Lauriston Castle'. He drove in slowly, paid and was given two tickets, then parked just beyond the lodge.

'I've never *heard* of it,' Lindy said as she got out. 'Lauriston Castle?'

'Oh, it's very old. Been here since twelve hundred and something, though not the same building. One day we'll go in and look at all the fine furniture and paintings, but today I want to show you the grounds.' He offered his arm, and led her up the drive, which curved through parkland dotted with trees and edged with laurel and rhododendron.

'This must be lovely when the bushes are in flower,' Lindy observed.

'It's always lovely. You'll see why in a minute. At least,' he added with that same look of momentary doubt, 'I hope you'll see it the way I do.'

They came to the castle, a grey stone edifice with pointed towers and high, wide windows. Lindy could see that a great deal of it had been altered or restored, but it was pleasing, especially framed in trees whose leaves were turned to gold. Rob led her round the side of the building, past a group of trimmed box and on to a croquet lawn, now deserted. She could see a path, with a few benches. He led her towards one of the benches. As they reached it, she saw the view.

The waters of the Firth of Forth stretched out before her like mottled grey-blue silk. On it a scattering of huge jewels seemed to float—seven islands, their green grass and brown rock gleaming under the autumn sun. A naval vessel was steaming out towards the North Sea, a feather of white wake streaming out behind her. Closer inshore, a score of sailing dinghies were deployed, their sails as gay as children's dresses—red, blue, orange, white and beige.

'*Oh!* Oh, but that's lovely. That's—that's—how perfectly lovely! I never imagined anything like this.'

He smiled. 'It's rather special, isn't it? That's why I don't bring anyone here unless they deserve it.'

'And you think I do?'

He nodded.

'I'm very flattered, Rob. I think you've paid me a great compliment.'

He sat down and patted the bench beside him. She sat down too.

'In a way, this is sort of an apology for being so rude to you that Sunday at Edinburgh Castle.'

She drew in a breath and let it go again—something more than a sigh but less than an exclamation: 'You were quite right in what you said. Anybody who could go on being in love with Lorenz would have to be silly and shallow.'

'I hear he's leaving.'

'Yes, the end of the month.'

'And you?'

She shrugged. 'I haven't made up my mind yet.'

'But he's asked you to go with him?'

That startled her. 'Good heavens, no. We haven't seen each other since the day of his " climb ". I thought you knew that.'

'What?'

'I thought most people knew. We haven't been seeing each other. He's going to Salzburg, I hear—but he's going alone.'

'I see.' There was a pause. 'Lindy . . .'

'Yes?'

'Why aren't you going with him?'

'He didn't ask me. And if he had, I'd have refused.' She cleared her throat. Here was the difficult part. 'You see, Rob, I discovered I'm not in love with him.'

He gave her a brief, sharp glance, then began to push at an inoffensive daisy with the toe of his shoe.

'But you were,' he remarked.

'Yes. I don't really know why. It was a bit like an illness. I got over it in the end.'

Rob hunched his shoulders. 'It couldn't have been a very deep emotion,' he said. 'One doesn't get over real love as easily as that.'

' No,' she acknowledged. ' You didn't, did you?'

He didn't look up. He leaned forward, picked the daisy, and ran his finger round it.

' " . . . Of all the flowers in the mead
    Than love I most these flowers white and rede," '

he quoted. ' I suppose it's because I spend all my time with exotic plants . . .'

She laid a hand on his arm and pulled him to face her. ' It's not like you to evade an issue,' she said, feeling a strange impulse of certainty. ' You still love me, don't you?'

He looked into her eyes, reading something there that seemed to please him. He covered her hand on his arm with one of his own.

' Arnold told you, didn't he, that I helped him get his post here at the University?'

' Yes, he did.' She was puzzled by this out-of-context question.

' He didn't tell you why.'

' Well, I suppose it was because—'

' He didn't tell you because he couldn't possibly know.' He stopped, frowned, then resumed. ' I like Arnold. For all his faults he's a nice chap. But the only reason I've bothered to stay friends with him all this while was because it was the only way to keep in touch, however remotely, with you.'

Although she heard the words and they made sense, Lindy couldn't quite seem to take them in. She turned her hand to link her fingers with Rob's.

' Do you think it was very underhand of me?' he asked, a quizzical tenderness in his voice.

' You could never be underhanded. I just feel . . . I'm just trying to take it in.'

' Does it seem so strange? Surely you knew I loved you, Lindy.'

' But that was two years ago. And I was so awful to you.'

He gave a little wry laugh. ' Yes, you were, weren't

189

you? And I was so angry. For quite a while I was angry. And then I realised that, angry or not, I was still in love with you.'

'It seems so *enduring*, Rob. To go on through two years without any encouragement.'

'There was encouragement of a sort in hearing that you were still single, that there was still a chance. And then came the news that you'd hurt your ankle. It seemed like news from heaven. I got Arnold moving at once.'

'You mean—*you* sent him to fetch me?'

He flushed. 'It makes me seem a real Machiavelli, doesn't it? I'm sorry. But I had to seize whatever chance I got.'

She was on the verge of saying, 'Don't be sorry.' But she caught back the words, for she had a question to ask. 'What about Marion?'

'What about her? Once Lorenz is gone she'll sort herself out.'

'You aren't in love with her? She says she always felt you were just being kind, but for a while I thought it was more than that.'

'Listen, be sensible. I couldn't love a girl who'd kill a whole hothouse-full of orchids.'

'You knew she'd done that and yet you didn't turn away from her. I thought that was love, Rob.'

He sighed. 'You remember her piano recital? When she hesitated on seeing you? I knew then—I'd only suspected her before. But . . . she was so unhappy, Lindy. And I know what it's like.'

'Oh, my darling!' She put up her hands to cup his face. 'Rob, forgive me for being so cruel and silly!'

He bent his head so that his lips met hers. It was a gentle kiss, almost hesitant—and she knew why. Once before in the past he had kissed her with passion, and she had recoiled. This time it was quite, quite different. She responded with her entire heart and soul, melting into his arms in a longing as deep as his own.

At last he let her go. She whispered, 'I don't deserve

t. I've been so stupid.'

'I won't let you say that about the woman I love.'

'Rob, my darling Rob . . . I must have been insane to run away from you two years ago.'

'Well, you know . . . Rare plants take some time in growing, don't they?'

'Do you think that was the reason? I was taking a great risk, though. You know that thing about Time withering the blossom—'

Rob quoted,

'"But Time did beckon to the flowers, and they
  By noon most cunningly did steal away,
  And withered in my hand."'

'That didn't happen. I was lucky—oh, so lucky, Rob. Not like poor Marion . . .'

'Marion will be all right,' he said. 'Arnold will look after her.'

'Arnold?' Lindy brought out her brother's name in a tone of utter disbelief. 'Arnold doesn't care . . .'

'Oh yes, he does. If you just watch, you'll see that Arnold has a habit of being around when Marion needs someone. In the end, she'll notice that. I shouldn't be in the least surprised if she ends up by marrying him.'

'I don't believe it! Arnold? He's never been in love in his life.' But then she remembered the talk she had had with him in the middle of the night, about love and marriage. There had been a wistfulness in his voice. And he had gone to see Marion on the day of the adventure on the Castle. 'Marion's gone with him this afternoon,' she said wonderingly, 'to help with his catalogue . . .'

'There, you see? You may be asked to do some wedding bouquets for Marion and Arnold quite soon!'

'That would be wonderful. Some of that lovely stephanotis of yours . . .'

Rob gathered her against him. 'Save some for your own bouquet,' he murmured. 'My dear love, I want you to make it soon . . .'

She lost herself in his embrace, totally his, totally happy. The lovely view from the bench was lost on them—but then they had opened a window on to Paradise itself.